BAD MONEY

Also by Ed Gorman in Large Print:

Branded
Breaking Up Is Hard to Do
Everybody's Somebody's Fool
Gun Truth
Lawless
Relentless
Ride into Yesterday
Save the Last Dance for Me
The Sharpshooter
Trouble Man
Ghost Town
Vendetta
Wake Up Little Susie
Will You Still Love Me Tomorrow?

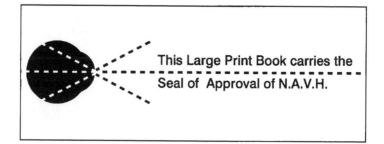

This Large Print Book carries the
Seal of Approval of N.A.V.H.

BAD MONEY

Ed Gorman

Thorndike Press • Waterville, Maine

Published in 2005 by arrangement with The Berkley Publishing Group, a division of Penguin Group (USA) Inc.

Thorndike Press® Large Print Western.

The tree indicium is a trademark of Thorndike Press.

The text of this Large Print edition is unabridged. Other aspects of the book may vary from the original edition.

Set in 16 pt. Plantin by Ramona Watson.

Printed in the United States on permanent paper.

Library of Congress Cataloging-in-Publication Data

Gorman, Ed.
    Bad money / by Ed Gorman.
        p. cm. — (Thorndike Press large print western)
    ISBN 0-7862-8153-7 (lg. print : hc : alk. paper)
    1. Counterfeiters — Fiction.   2. Secret service — Fiction.
3. Denver (Colo.) — Fiction.   4. Large type books.
I. Title.   II. Thorndike Press large print Western series.
PS3557.O759B33 2005
    813´.6—dc22   2005022870

To Bill and Judy Crider,
fine people and fine friends

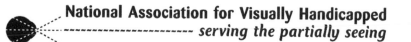

National Association for Visually Handicapped
-------------------- *serving the partially seeing*

As the Founder/CEO of NAVH, the only national health agency solely devoted to those who, although not totally blind, have an eye disease which could lead to serious visual impairment, I am pleased to recognize Thorndike Press★ as one of the leading publishers in the large print field.

Founded in 1954 in San Francisco to prepare large print textbooks for partially seeing children, NAVH became the pioneer and standard setting agency in the preparation of large type.

Today, those publishers who meet our standards carry the prestigious "Seal of Approval" indicating high quality large print. We are delighted that Thorndike Press is one of the publishers whose titles meet these standards. We are also pleased to recognize the significant contribution Thorndike Press is making in this important and growing field.

Lorraine H. Marchi, L.H.D.
Founder/CEO
NAVH

★ Thorndike Press encompasses the following imprints: Thorndike, Wheeler, Walker and Large Print Press.

I used many reference books and articles in writing the first Dev Mallory adventure. By far the most useful was *The Queen City: A History of Denver* by Lyle W. Dorsett, first published in 1977, a fine book with a sharp social eye. I took several liberties with the history I found, just as I took several liberties with the way the American monetary system was set up at the time. All mistakes are mine. As usual. Also, I'd like to thank Sue Reider for all her help.

— EG

An additional thank-you here to my editor, Samantha Mandor, for all her excellent advice.

PROLOGUE

From the Journal of Secret Service Agent Devlin Mallory

August 21, 1887

As near as I can figure, it took nearly twenty months for the criminals involved in the case to get it set up properly.

It started in Boston in September of 1886 and it started completely by coincidence. A special kind of burglar named George Watson, who was by trade a toolmaker and key fitter, had spent a long time developing his criminal craft. Watson would go into hotels, theaters, business offices, and other public places and snoop around to find where the janitor kept the keys to a particular building. Building managers and janitors usually seem to keep them in one place, frequently their own space in the basement or subbasement.

After combing the building to see which offices looked as if they'd yield the greatest treasures, Mason would sneak into where the keys were kept, make wax impressions of them, and then go to his home, where he would turn the impressions into keys.

He would then contact one of six burglary gangs and offer the keys up for auction. Whichever gang would give him the biggest cut would get the keys. Watson supported himself and his wife and nine children handsomely in this manner.

Then one night, a gang leader who had just broken into a basement printing plant with the help of a key he'd obtained from Watson told the key fitter what he'd found. Watson was intrigued enough by what he heard to mention it to an old friend who was passing through Boston at this time, one Vincent Kelly alias Louis Brockway alias Paul Fisher alias William Pease. Kelly was a swindler of some renown. He was also a man who saw his life as a quest for the ultimate swindle, one so vast in scope that it would allow him to live in luxury the rest of his life.

Kelly left Boston soon after, but his mind was already working to adapt to what he now believed would be the treasure he'd been looking for for so long.

As far as I can tell, that's how this particular case came into its slow and complicated beginning.

Two Months Earlier:

18 June 1887
Washington, D.C.

Dear Dev,
You'll notice that this isn't being written on official letterhead. Since I work for the Secret Service, as do you, I'm not sure how seemly it is to post a letter addressed to a house that is, in the parlance, a whorehouse.

Oh, yes, Dev, a couple of the boys and I went drinking one night over in Georgetown, and I was wondering aloud just how good ole Dev was doing on the three-day assignment so secret he couldn't even tell me about it. The lads started snickering like schoolboys. Told me you'd put in at some brand-new and very fancy whorehouse over in (God forbid) Alexandria. So that's your "secret."

Now, amusing as I find this, and I

do find it at least moderately amusing, I don't want it associated with our employer, one Grover B. Cleveland. I'm not sure he would find it amusing, not even moderately.

The last time I talked with him, he was in a bad mood. I talked to him about five minutes ago, in fact, so his mood isn't anything I've had time to forget, much as I'd like to. The phone is brand-new and is a direct dedicated line from the White House, just like the one Ted Phillips has at Treasury. I mention this so you won't try to call any whorehouses in the Washington, D.C., area when you come back here. You'll just end up talking to the President.

Given his mood — I want you back here within twenty-four hours and none of your bullshit. I don't even care if you've done something foolish, like fall in love with a tart.

Jubal Cartwright from the Bureau of Engraving and Printing, a man who never gets hysterical, got a private meeting with the President this morning and told him what's going on. The President, who does get hysterical and frequently, then called me on the private line and said that this could be the biggest queer scheme in our history, even bigger than what the Rebs tried in the war. You know how he distrusts several of the Secret Service men near the top. I'm told the Service has gotten ahold of this same scheme and is most unhappy that you — and this office — have been chosen to take it over. He asked specifically about you, since we're basically a consortium of freelancers. He remembers that late-afternoon tea he had for our British counterpart. You told him that the first counterfeiters were the Chinese in the 13th century. The government beheaded anybody caught manufacturing or trying to pass queer money. He thought it sounded like a damned good idea, which it is.

Anyway, put some clothes on and get back here posthaste. I assured everybody that you'd be on the case right away. I also told the President that Wally Tomkins — one of your best friends in the office here — stumbled on to the same scheme about two weeks ago. You'll be joining him in Denver and he can bring you up to *date. I've already bought your train ticket.*

Get your ass back here.

The Boss

PART ONE

Henry Juvenal Cummings

Henry Juvenal Cummings was the kind of person confidence men got down on their knees and prayed for. As did confidence women.

Dutifully married, the father of three grown children, a stern Lutheran, a staunch Freemason, a Northerner by birth but a Southerner in his soul (he'd been an enthusiastic Copperhead during the war), in the year 1886 Cummings was residing in a large house on Riggs Street NW in Washington with his wife Addie. Most of their social life was spent in the church basement where various "soirees," as the minister's wife liked to call them, were put on.

Two other factors played into Henry's ultimate fate. One was his promotion at the Bureau of Engraving and Printing. The other was his birthday. This was the year he turned forty-seven and for all the jokes he made about himself becoming old, he was besieged with a melancholy he couldn't rid himself of. He felt he'd misspent his life. He'd married at twenty, gone to work as an apprentice for a large printing shop in Ohio, and eventually worked his way to the nation's capital, where samples of his work got him a low-level job at Engraving. He'd risen steadily over the years until he was now one of the Bureau's key engravers.

He was thinking about how quickly and predictably his life had gone by on the sunny May afternoon when he saw the elegant lady stumble and drop her purse in the gutter.

Henry had been walking home from work, caught up in his thoughts, when this intruded on his quiet misery. Being a gentleman, he acted without thinking. He rushed to the purse, bent down, and swept it up. Only when he was handing the purse to the woman did he realize how fetching she was. Her face was a masterpiece of rich sexuality he'd only been able — guiltily — to dream of.

She was extravagantly proper. She accepted her purse the way royalty would accept a gift from a commoner. She terrified and intimidated Henry.

"It's so nice to meet a gentleman," she

said. Her voice was younger and softer than he would have imagined it. Perfect enunciation, of course. But still, open and friendly. "And such a nice-looking one at that."

Talk about your poleaxed middle-aged man. He couldn't speak. He knew he was blushing. No woman had complimented him since the earliest days of his courtship with Addie.

"Oh." She smiled. "I've embarrassed you. I'm sorry." Her chestnut-colored hair was the same color as her rich dark eyes.

And then she touched him. And that was all it was. A mere touch on the forearm. A mere *momentary* touch. Utterly meaningless. Except to Henry. He was a drab little bald man who until this very afternoon had been living in a miasma of self-pity and resignation. But the touch — her touch — opened him up to possibilities he'd only daydreamed of. He tried hard not to notice the swell of her breasts, the soft seductiveness of that full mouth, the playful self-confidence of those eyes. My God, my God. In this instant, he had been reborn. This fairy-tale princess had turned him into a youth again — in mind, body, soul, and groin he was a youth again!

He said, "There's an ice cream parlor

over there. Would you care for ice cream?"
Even though he'd spoken them, the words
weren't his somehow. He was just the
puppet, not the puppeteer.

But he knew as soon as he'd spoken that
she would say no. Being a proper lady, she
would be polite about it, but the answer
would still be no.

"Why, that sounds very good. One scoop
won't hurt me. I'm watching my diet, of
course, the way every other woman in this
city is." Washington had been infested with
diet plans this spring.

He wasn't sure he'd heard her correctly.
"You mean, yes?"

She laughed, and her laugh was sweet as
the apple blossoms blooming along the Po-
tomac just now. "Why, yes, I meant yes."

Only later that night, when he was
forced to lie to Addie — *working late,
dear; I'm sorry* — did the Lutheran in him
take over. He could have told her the truth,
of course. *Helped a young woman — she
reminded me a lot of our own Sally, dear
— and then she bought me an ice cream.
We just started talking. She's new here
and looking for a place to live and I
started describing the various neighborhoods and —*

This was the superficial truth, anyway.

18

The real truth was that he'd been trans-fixed. He was familiar with hypnotism — another recent Washington rage, especially at the parties of the elite in Georgetown — and wondered if she hadn't somehow taken over his mind and body. Because the real truth was now that he was home and seeing Addie and the house they lived in . . . That was when the Lutheran in him began to excoriate and damn him for the faithless fool he had suddenly become.

How old and fat sweet Addie looked; how colorless and frayed the house inside and out; how dull his nightly routine of meal — newspaper reading — eight-thirty bedtime. How he'd wasted his life.

But (argued the Lutheran) wasn't it possible that Addie felt the same way? What fun had she had in *her* life? Next year, she'd be forty-seven, too. Wouldn't she feel as estranged from herself as he did now?

He wanted to be fair, he wanted to be dutiful, he wanted to feel guilty about making plans to call on Claire Cherac (what a lovely French name; he'd said it over and over to himself on his guilty walk home tonight, after standing in the light from the ice cream parlor window and watching her disappear into the violet

19

shadows of dusk) at her hotel two days hence.

But even as he watched the lamplight play on Addie's plump cheek — she was of course in her favorite chair, reading a romance novel — he knew he could never walk away from the excitement that lay before him. Never.

ONE

The train was an hour late pulling into Denver. As I learned soon enough, that gave the killers plenty of time to take care of poor old Wally Tomkins. And pick his apartment clean while they were at it.

I'd known Wally in prison. I'd also recommended him for his job with the company. I wondered if, while they were cutting his throat, he'd had time to hate me for getting him into this. He'd had grandchildren back East. His plan was to retire in a year or so and buy himself a cottage near them.

They'd been damned neat about it. I'd never seen less mess with a throat-slashing. The collar and shirtfront were pretty well soaked, but I didn't see blood anywhere else. The stench came from his bowels.

In one of those odd little moments you sometimes have, I really looked at him for the first time. I'd never realized before how freckled his face was, nor how much hair shot from his nostrils, nor how deeply blue his eyes were. Poor old Wally. He'd spent his life in the same world we all had, the world of counterfeit money and forged documents. It never became a dangerous world until you signed on with the Boss.

Though I knew it was useless, I went through all the usual places in his furnished room. There were a few drawers hanging out but other than that, they'd been neat, almost fastidious in their search. Wally had damaged his lungs in the war. Every other drawer seemed to contain a patent medicine aimed at relieving his cough and his pain. It was hard to picture Wally without hearing his relentless cough.

I had to stop looking at one point because I heard footsteps coming up the stairs. Wally had one of two large apartments on the second floor of a very clean and comfortable Denver house. The footsteps went past, to the next apartment. A key was inserted into a lock and the footstep sound vanished. A well-built house.

What the killers hadn't known about was the heel on Wally's right shoe. The first time somebody at the company told me about it, I laughed. It sounded exactly like something out of those Nick Carter dime novels. Good old Nick had more gadgets than an entire Sears catalog.

Wally had always loved gadgets like his

specially designed shoes. The heel was built in two layers. The bottom layer swung out, if you knew the trick to doing it, and it was there you found the key to a strongbox in a local bank. Presumably, the strongbox held the agent's report. In case of his unexpected demise, another agent could easily find the report and take over the assignment. That heel was the largest contribution Wally had made to the company. In the larger scheme of things, I mean.

I'd arrived only two hours ago in Denver. I'd found a good hotel, stored my two bags, and then started looking for Wally. A very sweet young woman who lived down the hall had told me that she'd seen Wally go out about an hour ago. I'd thanked her and walked through the warm spring days patting dogs, smiling at kids, and quietly lusting after all the young mothers pushing their strollers. I'd found a café with decent coffee, had two cups, and then gone back to Wally's, where I'd found him as I described him earlier — dead, throat slashed.

The stench got a lot worse when I knelt down on one knee and pulled his shoe off. I carried the shoe over to the window and glanced out at the warm spring Denver afternoon. It was one of those cities that endlessly bragged about itself. And with good reason.

The heel wasn't cooperative. Whatever it had been designed to do, it wasn't doing it. I took out my pocketknife. The seven-inch blade tip sliced easily between the two sections of heel. Then the heel swung open.

On a tiny slip of paper the words CITIZENS SAVINGS BANK was written. A strongbox key engraved with the number seventy-three lay beneath the paper. I put the key in my pocket.

Getting Wally's shoe back on wasn't easy. He'd started to go stiff. I assumed that the counterfeiters had found out about him finding about them. Hence, his murder.

He had pretty formidable foot odor. I had to press close to finish twisting and turning his shoe on, and this smell was even stronger than the odor from his bowels. I don't recall the company ever mentioning moments like these when they were trying to entice me into a life of "selfless service," as one old Washington windbag had put it.

I gave Wally a jaunty little salute and left, stopping at the door down the hall where I'd spoken with the young woman.

She was probably twenty or so, a slender redhead with hazel eyes and a voice so soft you had to listen carefully. She wore a paisley dress that gently revealed her female splendors.

"Did you find Wally?" She'd introduced herself earlier as Nan Julian.

"I'm afraid I did."

" 'Afraid?' Why would you say that?"

"Somebody killed him."

I'd expected her to do all the things females do in books. To cry out, to put her hands over her face, maybe even to swoon and faint. She did none of them. She said, and quite simply at that, "He said they were after him. Poor Wally."

"Did he say who 'they' were?"

"No. Just that he'd found out about them and now they'd found out about him." Then she said: "Do you work for the same people Wally did?"

"Did he tell you who he worked for?"

"Not exactly. But he did tell me that he was a spy during the war. And that he got into some trouble and went to a Confederate prison with a man named Dev Mallory."

I nodded. So Wally, old and sick as he was, hadn't been able to resist telling tales of derring-do to this young woman. She had one of those innocent faces that invited your trust. Not to mention your carnal desires, too.

"Is that all he told you? I'm Mallory, by the way."

"Why, yes, he said he wasn't at liberty to

25

tell me more. I invited him in for dinner several times. We were both alone and I really enjoy cooking after a long day at the store — Wendale's Women's Ware — that's how we got to know each other. Poor Wally. He was such a good friend." Her expression changed. "Oh, Lord, they wouldn't come after me, would they?"

"Why would they come after you?"

"Well, you know — because Wally talked to me all the time."

"I'm pretty sure you'll be fine."

"I'm from a small town up in the mountains. My dad gave me one of his old pistols. I guess this is the time to load it. I'm sorry if I sound scared but —" She shrugged. "Well, I guess I *am* scared."

"I'll be back. I noticed a police call box two corners down. If you're nervous, don't answer the door until you're sure it's me."

"Could we have a code or something like that?"

She had to be a reader of magazine romances. This season they were filled with dashing spies who used codes for virtually everything.

"Sure," I said. "I'll knock twice and then say 'Old Glory.' "

"Old Glory. That's perfect."

26

TWO

According to the Eastern newspapers, this Denver of 1887 was the most elite and modern city in the west. When the gold mines started to tap out, high-grade silver ore was discovered. Not to mention over three thousand miles of railroad track and the largest downtown area outside of San Fran itself.

Those newspaper assessments were hard to argue with if you stayed downtown, the centerpiece of which was the three-hundred-room Windsor Hotel that had three elevators and a vast ballroom. If you wanted to see how local royalty lived, you rode your horse or took a trolley past the three areas where the rich had their mansions. None of this would have been so offensive to the average man if the Denver businessmen hadn't decided to keep wages for all jobs as low as possible. They wanted to attract more and more manufacturing, which was sensible enough as long as you weren't one of the workers. Denver was a place dedicated to making fortunes for those who

27

had fortunes already. It wasn't inclined to correct social ills.

Sewer construction was going on in several places. Despite all its gleaming pride, Denver was a pretty smelly place. Waste of all kinds — industrial, stockyard, human waste — was dumped into the Platte River, making for some pretty memorable odors. Then there were the dogs. Packs and droves of them. The city paid a twenty-five-cent bounty on them. The shooters rarely chased the animals they'd only wounded. As a result, you got even more smells as many of the animals managed to survive for a few days and then died in place, making even more of a stench. So many wounded dogs could be seen — dogs with their guts hanging out, dogs blinded in one eye, even pregnant dogs spilling out their unborn — that a citizens' committee rose up and got the town council to ban the practice. But then a year after the ban went into effect, dog packs began attacking schoolchildren and the shooters got busy again. More carcasses, more smells to add to the dead horses, mules, swine that were everywhere, too.

Six blocks south of the downtown, you started to see the men and women who hadn't — by choice or chance — shared in Denver's success. The hobos and the derelicts and the crazy people that the city fathers had made no provision for. The worst were the kid gangs. Boys and girls from six to sixteen. Helping their parents scrape together a living by any means necessary, which usually meant purse snatching, burglary, or robbery. Hard to forget them, especially at twilight when their dirty faces and ragged clothes lent them wild-animal looks — a species of animal not quite human — as they waited for darkness to start preying on drunks and whores and small scared citizens who had to hurry through the streets that the gangs controlled.

Fortunately for everybody, there were parts of the town's center where every day was Easter Sunday. I hadn't seen this many peacocks, women and men alike, since my last trip to New York City. Top hats and spats for the men; bustles and huge picture hats for the women. I ate an early lunch in the window of a small café that catered to the peacock and peacockettes. I alternated between watching them on the street and watching all the types of vehicles that passed through the center of town. I was reminded of New York again, the great hum and hurry of success and riches. Sunlight bled like molten gold off the large windows of all the fancy shops and stores. Even the lazy dust motes, climbing up in the wake of a coach's passing, gleamed like gold.

I saw a Cinderella-like coach pull up in front of a massive stone storefront. The woman who emerged from it, on the arm of a gentleman twice her age, was so regal-looking I wanted to kneel down on one knee and kiss her hand. Maybe later we could get around to kissing other parts of her perfect body.

Walking into the bank was akin to having a religious experience. The vaulted marble ceiling, the marble pillars, the long line of teller windows that could have been confessionals, and the whispered reverence of the bank staffers when they spoke to customers lacked only incense and a choir to make the experience complete. The newspaper cartoonist who'd coined the term "The Almighty Dollar" hadn't been far wrong.

I'd come here directly from Wally's apartment. I'd spent two hours with the police. I'd used my usual cover story, which was that I was a writer and that

Wally was an old friend. Nan Julian's romance with codes and mysterious deaths had faded. She lay on her mussed warm bed and wept for better than an hour. I sat on the edge of the bed for a time, rubbing her back and shoulders until her rather resplendent backside began to suggest thoughts not appropriate to this moment. Sometimes my crotch begins to exert a stronger influence on me than my brain. That always leads to trouble. When the police were done with me, I grabbed a trolley and went downtown.

I went to the back of the bank where a door said SECURITY BOXES. A bald pudgy guard of many decades sat in a chair next to the door. What appeared to be a standard Colt .45 was holstered to his side. He blew on the surface of his hot coffee and watched me approach at the same time. He had suspicious eyes the color of dirty water.

What he saw was a slim city man whose black hair was just starting to turn gray. A dark city suit of medium cost. A face a few kind ladies have called handsome. And a manner that reflects a Dartmouth College education and many seasons of running confidence games in and around Washington, D.C. During the war, these games were legal. I was a Yankee spy. The trouble came when I couldn't seem to give up the games after the war.

"Afternoon," the guard said.

"Afternoon. I'd like to see my security box."

He studied me. "I'm pretty good at faces."

"Remembering them, you mean?"

"That's right," he said, keeping his scrutiny intense. "Remembering them. And I've worked here a long time."

"This must be what that sign 'Friendly Service' means on the front window." I showed him my key. "Walter Tomkins. I'm in sort of a hurry."

He set his coffee down on a small magazine-covered side table and stood up. "Your face still ain't registering. You have some sort of identification?"

I pulled out Wally's identification papers and handed them over.

He scanned them, handed them back. "You're Wally Tomkins, huh?"

"That would seem to be the case."

He handed my identification back. He gave the sense of easing up on his suspicions. He'd probably figured out that if I went to see his boss, and the boss believed the identification papers I handed him, he was in trouble with the whole notion of friendly service.

"I'm really in a hurry," I said.

He offered me a smile that seemed to take a great deal of work to muster up. "Sorry if I was a little suspicious there. I'm just doing my job. I didn't mean to insult you none."

He'd been too unfriendly when I approached. Now he went into a subservient routine that made both of us feel awkward.

"That's fine. I just need to get into my security box."

"Sorry to hold you up, sir."

The door opened on a large room lined with strongboxes. There were four stand-up counters where the boxes could be set and the contents examined.

Two keys were required to open each box. Each of us inserted keys at the same time.

"There you go, sir," he said. "I'll be right outside the door if you need anything." He was still nervous about being so suspicious of me. "Sorry about not recognizing you. Just doing my job."

"And I appreciate that. Knowing that you don't slough off."

He smiled. "Thanks for saying that, sir."

"My pleasure."

He left. I opened the box and found what I was looking for. The report was dated last night. Six pages of cramped but readable penmanship.

What I was expecting was the usual thing. Though the Wild West was no longer so wild, there was one aspect of it that had yet to be tamed and that was regulating its finances. Up until last year, you still had wildcat banks that printed their own currency; crooked banks that were set up for the sole purpose of going broke after customer money had been shipped safely out of state or even out of country; and massive counterfeiting scams that were often tied to antigovernment groups. The latter folks figured that the fastest way to bring down a government was to undermine the integrity of its currency. Parts of the Confederacy were still at war, just as the Jayhawkers had been after the surrender was signed. Both sides had acted admirably and despicably.

As I read through Wally's report, I remembered why I'd been ordered to come out here in the first place. Wally had needed help. . . .

Once upon a time there was a man named Henry Cummings, who was one of the official engravers of United States paper currency. One day four weeks ago, my boss in Washington called me in to talk about Cummings. Cummings was a quiet man who spent his off hours playing with his two grandchildren and collecting German beer steins. He also collected first editions of Jules Verne. He rarely drank, had never chased the ladies, and ushered at his Lutheran church every Sunday morning. Not the sort of upstanding man our agency usually dealt with.

We were talking about all this one warm afternoon, not long after I'd been retrieved from the bawdy house in Alexandria, in a fastidiously kept office in the nation's capital. The Boss and I were talking, I mean.

I should tell you about the Boss. The blue glass eye in the right socket? Happened on a steamboat when a Confederate saw the Boss breaking into a passenger room. It's one of those manly stories that I'd doubt coming from anyone else of the male persuasion. The way the Boss tells it, he was so angry about his eye being ripped out with a knife that he tore the other man's eyes out with his own fingers, smashed the man's head against a pillar until the man was dead, and then threw him overboard. The Boss opted for a glass eye instead of an eye patch.

"Now we have a new problem," the Boss said. "Two months ago Henry Cummings — who'd been in charge of designing two of the new pieces of paper money — disappeared from Washington. He left work at the normal time and was never seen again. His wife and his coworkers said that he gave no indication he was unhappy. That doesn't necessarily mean anything, of course. A lot of men vanish when they seem happy and content. But this leaves us with two possible trails to look for Henry Cummings. One, he was kidnapped. Or two, he just walked away. Maybe he had a lady friend. Maybe he just found his life stifling. Whatever happened, I think you can see what this might possibly mean."

The Boss unbuttoned his vest. His suit coat was hung on the back of his leather business chair. I'd never seen him actually wear a suit coat. He just carried them to and from work, I think. I suppose if the President came over here — which he never would — the Boss would put his jacket on. Otherwise, I couldn't imagine him actually wearing one. That would conflict with the wrinkled and rumpled look he seems to cultivate and cultivate quite successfully, even though his clothes are custom-tailored and expensive. He usually looks as if he'd just been kicked out of a jail cell for drunks.

"He might go into business for himself," I said. "He could print some beautifully bad money."

He reached into his inner pocket again. Took out two pieces of paper currency. Laid them on his desk side by side. "Guess which one's queer. You're good at this, Dev. But try it with these."

I spent five minutes doing all the expected things with the bills, finishing up with a magnifying glass.

I finally sat back and said, "I don't see any difference."

"The right lower corner of the backside."

I went over it again. After a minute: "I'll be damned. That tiny faded spot. I'm not even sure you could measure it."

"It's the paper. Washington contacted every place that sold paper even remotely similar to the paper it uses. These paper mills were ordered to tell us immediately if anybody asked for it. There's a mill in Baltimore that produces a paper that's very close to the official stuff. They gave us the address of the man who'd ordered it. He ordered it from Denver. The name he used was Ted Nealon. He obviously had beautiful plates, but the paper tripped him up."

"I'd pass it right through. I wouldn't hesitate. Even with the bad paper, it's the best counterfeiting I've ever seen."

"That's what makes him so dangerous. When a man like you can't spot it, we have a big problem. By now, I'm assuming he's gotten his hands on better paper. If he has Henry Cummings helping him, he'll be in excellent shape for everything — paper, ink, and certainly the plates. I'm told Cummings has knowledge of virtually every aspect of producing paper money."

"I take it you haven't found him yet."

"No, not yet. But Wally Tomkins has been wiring me. He thinks he's found the counterfeit ring producing this money. And the money's so good, he thinks that Cummings is involved. He doesn't think anybody except Cummings could make plates like these." He made a face. "And there's something else. Something very odd."

I rolled a cigarette and listened.

"Wally says there were seven people in this ring when it started. But that two of them have been murdered in the past few weeks. He has no idea who is killing these people or why. But he said that from what he can see, the group is scared. It would be logical that someone in the remaining group is the killer. Maybe killers, plural. They want more for themselves. But Wally isn't sure about that. And neither is the group."

"You want me to find the killer?"

He shook his head. "I don't give a damn what happens to scum like that. I'm just giving you all the background I can. The two things I want you to do is find Cummings and the plates and bring them both back here. Find the plates and you're likely to find Cummings. And vice versa. But you'd better find them both damned fast before they decide to start passing this queer stuff all over the West."

Four hours later, I was on a westbound train packed tight with pickpockets, bratty kids, drunkards, soul-savers of the most obnoxious kind, pukers, snorers, nose-pickers, ass-scratchers, and all-purpose skin-rashed, blackheaded, runny-nosed, scum-teethed folk I couldn't help but feel sorry for. They were headed west, cheap cloth bags filled with nothing but day-dreams and frail nervous hopes. Six months from now, a pretty good share of them would be in prison, in asylums, or in graveyards.

The rest of the afternoon, after finding Wally's body and going to the bank, I stayed in my room. I took a nap because train sleep is never good sleep. And then I went back to Wally's report.

At dusk, a starry, wine-red sky and an early half-moon cast a kind of alien melancholy over the city. I went to the hotel restaurant and had a good meal, my first since leaving Washington.

I knew what I was going to do, something I did in most of my travels, and out of necessity not choice.

I asked one of the bellboys where I'd find the cleanest girls in town. I'd had one bout with scabies. I didn't want any more.

THREE

"He wouldn't be doin' that if Miss Darla was here."

She was probably not much older than twenty, and judging from the way she kept trying to cover herself up, she hadn't been at it long. Her name was Amy and she was from a Kansas farm and she wasn't sure this was the right thing to do but so far it hadn't been too bad. It was better than having her pa beat on her, she said.

There's one thing I've noticed about some prostitutes. They like to talk about themselves. Usually they're sad stories meant to justify the lives they're leading. Sometimes their stories are so vivid, they get you out of the mood and the girls have to spend time reviving your interest. At least with me, anyway.

Amy, tonight, had given me the three-minute biography. And that was just dandy. Three minutes are required to get undressed, roll a cigarette to smoke for afterward, and ease yourself into a comfortable position in bed. The trick is to pretend you're listening. Jump in any-where. Ask a question. Then she thinks you're paying full attention. No sense in hurting feelings.

But it wasn't Amy's jabber that was getting in the way tonight. It was a drunkard.

"All the girls're afraid they'll have to take Earle some night. He's real scary."

The house was a new Victorian, fussy in fake British decoration, but kempt and clean. You could smell apple blossoms through the open window. The room was on the second floor of a crib where, the bellboy had assured me, a real M.D. doctor checked these girls out once a month.

A friend of mine said that he gave up screwing faces a long time ago, meaning he doesn't care if they're pretty or not as long as they know how to sex him. I'm more along the lines of a sentimental fool, I guess. I like the pretty ones, and the gentle ones, and the soft-spoken ones. A lot of whores, they get to be a whole lot rougher and tougher than the men they're putting out for.

"Miss Darla is the madam?" I said there in the dark.

"Uh-huh. Her sister's real sick. So she's stayin' with her a couple days. She left Nancy in charge, but Nancy's just as afraid of Earle as we all are."

42

I was down to my underwear and about to climb into bed. "You mean this could go for a while?"

"You mean the screaming?"

"Uh-huh."

"That's not as bad as when he slaps her. That's how my pa used to slap me like that. Every time he slaps her, I can feel it."

She looked afraid even talking about it, her small face tight in the faint light of the turned-down lamp.

"I'll be back."

"Where you going, mister? Earle's about three times your size. They say he fought a bear once."

She squinted into the shadows to see what I'd lifted from the trousers I'd draped over the chair.

"What's that, mister?"

"They call it a sap. Some do, anyway. Other folks call it a blackjack. Now you stay right there."

A couple of the girls were in the hall. One of them was crying and holding the other one. "She'll be all right, Louise."

"She's my sister."

They were young girls, modest in their wrappers, awkward in their fear.

Both girls watched the door of the room where Earle was now whaling away.

43

I went up to them and whispered, "I need a good length of rope. And I need a bandanna. Fast."

"You going in there?" Louise asked.

"Just get me the rope."

I took training with the Marines. The Boss insisted on it. He'd been a Marine himself and believed, as Marines mostly do, that no other branch of service compares to them in the efficiency and skill it takes to kill a man. The training has helped keep me alive more than once. But so has my trusty sap. I don't fight by rules; I fight to survive and to inflict maximum pain, death if necessary, though there isn't nearly as much of that as the press would lead you to believe in companies such as ours. Murder has a way of coming back after you. The man you kill tonight may have a brother who comes after you a year from now and shoots you in your sleep.

I backed up as far as I could, hunkered down the way I used to when I played football. I charged the door. The damned thing ripped right off its hinges.

A naked girl was crouched on the bed. I took time to note her breasts, which were pretty darned amazing.

Earle was just about to slap her across the face, but then stopped in mid-motion when he received a dim drunken signal from his brain that somebody had just smashed through the door.

He was big, all right. Six-five, two-fifty. What I hadn't expected was that he was a refined gent. He wore silk drawers and sock garters and had, for some reason, kept an expensive gray derby on his head. I'd expected a sweaty saloon bully.

He was too big to fight fair. He turned and started staggering toward me. He was too drunk to move quickly, which was my biggest advantage. I grabbed a whiskey bottle from the bureau and smashed it across his face. The pain of that stalled him long enough for me to bring the toe of my Texas boot up and get him square in the groin. He was like a wall collapsing.

When he was down and mostly out, I hit him four times with the sap. I was careful where I put the hits. There are at least a couple thousand thugs in prisons who underestimated the killing potential of saps.

The girls were there with the rope. While Louise guided her sobbing sister out of the room, I got our friend Earle trussed up and gagged.

Amy appeared. "What're you going to do with him?"

"Well, being that it's nearly three in the morning, I thought I might spend the rest of the night here and then untie him when I leave."

"God, mister, you didn't kill him, did you?"

"Not that I know of."

"Good. Because I guess I should've mentioned that his father is the chief of police."

"I'm glad you got around to pointing that out." I looked down at Earle. I had him so bound up you could barely see his head. Naturally, I wasn't thrilled about his old man being a copper. But there wasn't much I could do about it now.

I left him in the room, closed the door, and went back to the bed we'd been occupying. Her skin was silken and her small breasts had just the kind of large, chewy nipples I like. She made love like a civilian not a whore, even flattering me a little afterward. I, of course, did my part in the play and flattered her right back.

We made love a second time, more quietly than the first time, and then she lay her prairie girl head on my arm and slept, making tiny snoring sounds the way a kitten does.

I was just starting to fall asleep when

Earle kicked the door open and started blasting away with two six-guns. He looked pretty silly there in his silk drawers and garters. He'd even managed to get his derby back on.

The first thing I did was grapple for my gun in the half-light from the sconces in the hall. The second thing I did was take my foot and kick Amy off the far side of the bed, so that she landed on the floor. "Crawl under the bed!" I shouted.

The third thing I did — and you have to understand that these things all happened in less than twenty seconds — was throw myself off the other side of the bed. I started rolling toward a stout bureau of dark wood in the east corner of the room.

He was too drunk to shoot carefully. But he wasn't drunk enough to empty his guns. He had several bullets left, and it was clear he meant to use them well. The house had once again exploded with screams, curses, otherwise respectable gents grabbing their Stetsons and derbies and heading the hell out the back door.

Earle's next shot just about did me in. After I heard him trip against a rocking chair, I leaned my head out no more than an inch past the edge of the bureau. He got lucky. Moonlight and hall light conspired to give him a clear look and thus a clear shot at me. He still looked damned silly in his derby and drawers and garters. But that didn't inhibit him from just about killing me.

I ducked back behind the bureau. Another wait ensued.

"What's going on in there?" demanded a female voice in the hall. The voice was out of breath from coming up the stairs.

"They're trying to kill each other," said Louise.

"Is it that damned Earle?"

"Yes."

"Well, I hope he gets his ass shot off. I'm sick of him takin' advantage just because his old man's the chief of police around here."

"Sounds like you got a lot of friends, Earle," I shouted at him. And he responded just the way I'd hoped he would. He took three more shots at me. But he didn't come close. He was a bad shot drunk; drunk and mad, he was a hopeless shot. By my unreliable count, he was now down to two bullets.

"I hear you beat up women because you just can't get that little pecker of yours to stand up straight," I said.

You can insult a man's bank account,

looks, even his religion, and in the right mood he'll cut you a little slack and walk away. But you can't insult his sexual acumen. That is sacred territory. His manhood is on the line and he'll punish you in the worst way he can think of.

He fired once.

Did he have a bullet left or was my count off?

"Maybe we should get the police," somebody in the hall said.

"Miss Darla'll be mad if we do."

"We can't just let 'em kill each other."

"Sure we can. The chief don't like that stupid son of his any more than we do."

"You know, Earle, those women keep running you down the way they do, I'll end up feelin' sorry for you," I said. "You're not man enough to please a woman and now even your pop doesn't like you. You're a pretty sad cowpoke, Earle."

"You shut up!" he shouted. "You can ask any damned girl I ever screwed about my pecker. I got one of the biggest peckers in the county. And my old man likes me just fine. You just ask him!"

Then he squandered what I counted as his last bullet. All he got for his trouble was a piece of wall two feet above my head.

I almost did feel sorry for him. I'd been

where he was enough times to know the frenzy, the rage, the disorientation of being drunk and wanting to kill somebody. Of being sad and foolish and pathetic and dangerous all at the same time. But he was a woman-beater and when I remembered that, any pity I might have felt for him was gone.

But I didn't want to kill him. The local law can make life hell for somebody like me. Even if Earle's old man didn't like him much — and it wasn't hard to see why he might not — if I killed Earle, his old man would hunt me down till his final breath.

"How you doing under the bed?" I said to Amy.

"I need to pee."

"So do I," I said.

"I mean really bad."

"Same here. But first I've got to take care of Earle."

"I can hear you talkin' about me, Amy. I'm gonna give you one of my black eyes next time I get my hands on you."

"You're not gonna do jack shit to anybody, Earle," I said. I stood up from the desk. I sure hoped my count was right. I sure hoped he'd fired his last round. "Now drop that gun. It's empty, anyway."

"The hell if it is."

"The hell if it isn't."

I had my gun on him and he had his gun on me. I was under the impression that mine was the only one with a bullet in it.

"You wanna try me?" Earle said.

"Look, you stupid-ass drunk, you make me shoot you, I just might end up killing you. Now put the gun down. And right now."

"Earle," Amy said from under the bed, "I really do need to pee. And really bad."

"I'm sick of both of you!" Earle shouted.

And that was when he fired. He was so reeling drunk by now that he missed me by two feet again, this time smashing up the mirror.

He might have had another bullet left, but at this point I didn't give a damn. I just jammed my gun back into its holster and dove across five feet of empty space. I grabbed him hard enough around the hips to throw him back several feet against the wall. I didn't give him time to collect himself. I jumped on him and started pounding away. The punches hurt my hands pretty bad but I kept going anyway, nose-jaw-forehead-jaw. I think I did a little strangling, too, as long as I was down near the throat. And then I threw in some head-banging against the wall. I kept thinking about poor old Walt Tomkins. Earle probably hadn't had anything to do with Walt's death, but right now facts didn't matter. All I needed was a face to punch in.

I never have figured out what the ladies hit me with. I have the impression that it was metal and expensive, though, because right before I fell unconscious to the floor, I heard Louise say, "Miss Dana's gonna be pissed off you hit him with that, Lurleen."

While I waited alone in the police reception area the next morning, I read through a brochure the coppers had done about themselves. Their uniforms, with their flashy badges and gleaming brass buttons and fancy caps, were modeled after those of the New York City police. There was a group picture of the current crop of coppers, a somber lot, each bearing an imposing mustache. Because the city was growing so quickly, the cops now went on horseback as well as foot. Within the past two years all criminals known to reside within the city limits had been photographed. This past year patrol wagons were put into service. There were thirty police telephone call boxes in the city. The coppers now called for a wagon to pick up their crooks. No more goading the crook at gunpoint half the way across the city to the station. Now he could sit in the comfort of a coffin on wheels that smelled of sweat, piss, liquor, beer, puke, and horseshit. All the pleasures of home.

I hoped the Denver police were a more lawful bunch than their Chicago counterparts, six hundred of whom had been fired in a single day for various felonies that led to an editorial with the headline THE FINEST COPS MONEY CAN BUY. The Boss had thumbtacked this to his bulletin board. Come to think of it, the Chicago coppers' uniforms were just like those worn by the Denver coppers.

When the chief came through the door, I couldn't believe he was the chief at all. It's an old theater gag probably dating back to at least the Middle Ages and the Italian comedies. First you have the son come on stage, and he's huge and strapping and threatening. And then you bring the father on stage, and he's half the size of his progeny.

He was small, trim but fierce. The eyes were especially nasty, cold and black and utterly without mercy. He wore a khaki uniform like those favored by British Army officers, right down to the small slash of gray mustache and magnificent riding boots that came up to his knees. You would make a terrible mistake if you thought this small man couldn't kill you. And I mean with his bare hands.

He led me back down the hall to his office, went behind his desk, and sat down. He had all the framed photographs you'd expect a city official to have. Chief Clement Yancy greeting locally famous people, usually shaking hands in that posed way they have. The trouble is, you got five miles outside the city limits, in any direction you care to name, and the celebrity of these folks vanished. Who the hell were they, anyway?

He picked up a pipe. He didn't light it, didn't even put it in his unhappy slash of mouth. He just rolled the gnarled briar over and over in his hands, studying it with hands that would have been large on a man twice his size. I noted several smashed knuckles.

He said, "We've got two things to talk about here today."

"Oh."

"My detectives tell me you found the body of your friend, a Mr. Tomkins."

"That's right."

"The doctor said he died before your train arrived. That clears you of the murder, but it doesn't clear you of the fact that you were very vague when you talked to the detectives about how you knew Tomkins in the first place."

"The war. That's how I knew him. I told them that."

"And that's about all you told them. You told them you didn't know what he did for a living, you didn't know why anybody would be after him, and you took the liberty of picking his lock because you had a 'bad feeling' about everything. Very vague stuff, Mr. Mallory. I don't suppose you'd care to add to it a little bit — or even do the unthinkable and actually tell me the truth?"

"I told you the truth."

"Of course you did."

He sat forward in the chair. "Well, no use wasting any more time on that particular topic. We'll just have to see how things play out over the next few days. See who this Tomkins was and what he was doing in Denver. Now, I'm going to change the subject, Mr. Mallory."

"Your son Earle."

"My son Earle."

"Do you want my side of it, Chief?"

He rested his elbows on his desk and said, "I could put you in county lockup for a long time, Mr. Mallory." His voice was as dead and cold as his gaze.

"I guess you could. But then I'd get a lawyer."

"Don't start this bullshit. I don't like threats. Especially where there's no need for one. I was just making the point that I have a little more influence in this town than you do. Technically, you broke the law just by being in that whorehouse. Not to mention carrying a sap."

"How about your son beating up on women and then firing on me?"

He frowned. "This is exactly what I don't want to waste my time on. All these charges and countercharges. I'm not a judge. I'm a police officer. I was a major in the war. And I learned to keep things simple. Now shut up and let me finish."

I shut up.

"I said that I *could* — if I wanted to — put you in lockup for a long time. I'd have to finesse a few laws, get a couple of felons to make up some good stories and testify against you, and then stick you down a hole for six months and forget you." He stuck his pipe in his mouth. He didn't light it. "But somewhere down the line, that would only complicate things. So here's what I'm prepared to do. Drop the charges against you for pounding on Earle if you'll forget all about Earle shooting at you."

"He's the worst shot I've ever seen. Two guns at six, seven feet at most. And he still couldn't kill us?"

"I'm not here to discuss marksmanship, Mallory. I'm offering you a swap. Your freedom for forgetting about Earle's shooting at you. If I wanted to, I could say that he was only responding to the beating you'd given him."

"And I was only responding to the beating he'd given the girl."

He took the pipe from his mouth. "Think it through, Mallory. No crib girl is going to testify against a citizen unless it's on a felony murder charge. For one thing, women who run whorehouses work at the mercy of the police department."

"Because they pay off the police department."

"That wouldn't be any of your business, Mallory. The point is, nobody who works at that crib is going to testify against Earle. Not even the girl you claim he beat up. So there goes your side of the case right there."

I smiled. "Neat. The city doesn't learn about how your son likes to beat up whores and I don't spend six months down the hole, as you put it."

"Exactly."

I shrugged. "I couldn't say no to that."

"Fine," he said, and leaned back in his chair. He stared at me a long moment and then said, "Who are you, Mallory?"

"Meaning what exactly?"

"Meaning that we went through everything in your hotel room. You apparently came here from Washington, D.C. That's what your train ticket says, anyway. And the same for three newspapers we found in your suitcase. Washington, D.C. That's bound to make a naturally suspicious man like me even more suspicious. Would you happen to be with the Justice Department?"

"I'm a writer, Chief. Didn't you see my articles when you went through my bag?"

"I saw them, all right. . . . All nice and neat in a little stack. But that doesn't mean you actually wrote them."

"You're a trusting soul. Would you like to stand over me the next time I'm writing?"

"You're staying at the Metropole."

"Yes, and really enjoying it."

"Pretty expensive, though. Mark Twain always talks about how hard it is to make a living writing."

"Business has been good."

"You're a bullshit artist, Mallory, and I

detest bullshit artists. Especially ones who seem to take pride in it. I'm not an excessive man, Mallory. I try not to hold grudges or single people out for observation or incarceration. But I'm telling you to be careful while you're here. I might find it difficult to be fair to you. And that wouldn't be good for either one of us."

"Especially me."

He stood up. Came around the desk. "I'm glad my son didn't kill you."

"For my sake or his?"

"Very good question, Mallory. For his sake, of course." The hard face got harder. "I'd hate to arrest my only child for murder."

FOUR

The city had an excellent library. I spent three hours there gathering as much material as I could on the five names that Wally had listed as part of the counterfeiting ring.

MR. AND MRS. LAWRENCE K. KIMBLE

Kimble was the president of the bank where Wally had kept his safety deposit box. When the group met, Mrs. Kimble was always present.

ARTHUR K. DAVIS

Davis was a highly paid tort attorney who was rumored to be part of a seditionist group that had tried unsuccessfully to launch a huge counterfeit ring before.

TED NEALON

A former whoremaster, confidence

man with, it is suspected, at least three murders in his past.

SERENA HOPKINS

A spoiled rich girl who'd squandered her inherited fortune on bad investments her friend Arthur K. Davis had warned her against.

Wally's assumption had been that one, some, or all of this group knew where Henry Cummings was. And thus knew where the counterfeit plates were. Reasonable enough. He also believed that one or two of them — now that the entire enterprise was set up and just about ready to go — was killing off other members of the group. None of the group could go to the police and ask for protection. They would have to explain their part in the counterfeiting.

My problem would be meeting them. There was only one way in for me and that was my guise as a writer. Most people were flattered to be written about and thus didn't ask many questions about my background. I had a dozen articles in good magazines to show them as examples of my work. The Boss had had them dummied up for me in a print shop in Georgetown where all sorts of printed materials were forged and faked.

I decided that the best place to start was one of the newspapers. Local journalists were usually friendly to me. For the price of a cup of coffee, they'd tell me all kinds of things about their towns and their fellow citizens, especially if I'd tell them about the world of magazine writing. I suppose it sounded exotic compared to working the same beat. But then I couldn't say. Like a number of things in my life, the magazine writing claim was a fraud.

"Well, to put it in simple terms, the important families here keep intermarrying, so that most of the power stays in the hands of just a few dozen people. And that isn't likely to change anytime soon, Mr. Mallory."

He was pure Western journalist. Busted nose, boozy eyes, tobacco hack. Sleeves of a soiled white shirt rolled up; typewriter in the middle of battered desk; papers, books, magazines stacked all around his typewriter; and an ashtray that hadn't been emptied since Lee surrendered. His name was Jay Carney, he openly spiked his coffee with a pint of rotgut, and since he worked for the city's only labor paper, he addressed the elite with a mixture of scorn and amusement.

"The pattern is they get sent to prep school, then they go to Harvard or Yale, and then they come back here and join the Colorado Club and spend the rest of their lives cheating, raping, and spiritually murdering the working class. They've even been known, from time to time, to have people killed. Sometimes the great unwashed can't take it anymore and they get uppity, and then the hired thugs move in to take care of them."

The labor papers promote their own point of view, but that point of view tends to be closer to reality than the big official papers that are run by and for the gentry.

The Messenger offices were on the second floor of a building on the edge of the area where poor whites made walking at night a very dangerous passage. There were maybe ten people rushing around, getting the twice-weekly paper ready for printing. Carney sat like an Irish Buddha in the center of the mayhem, serene in his rage against the rich.

"How about the people on the list I just handed you?" I said.

I had to speak loudly. A couple of dogs

had wandered into the newsroom and one of them had taken to barking. "Shut up, Curly!" Carney shouted at him. "Or no more booze for you!" Curly, standing beneath a large poster saying STRIKE! showing the photograph of two miners lying dead in the street, shot Carney a look of total dismissal.

"I call them strivers, the ones you list here," Carney went on. "They're not 'first tier' as the important people like to call themselves. They're second or third tier trying to make it to first. They never will, of course. The rich see that kind of open ambition as embarrassing — unless it's their own, of course. But they're useful to the rich in various ways. Take our friend Lawrence Kimble. If a rich man needs some corners cut in a business deal, he'll go to Kimble. He runs money through his bank for a pretty large number of old rich folks — mostly of the male persuasion and mostly of the male persuasion that have tarts stashed somewhere for their private amusement. Nothing illegal at all. But devious. I suppose Kimble thinks he's piling up points with these folks, but he's not. Oh, Kimble and his wife get invited to a party at the rich man's home once in a while. The rich man gets what he wants and Kimble and his wife get to brag that they went to so-and-so's party. And this translates into dollars because Kimble has been to enough of these parties that he's seen by all the other strivers as an important man." He smiled. "I wish I could say that this only went on in Denver, but it goes on in every city, town, and village in the world. Human nature, I guess."

"Same with Arthur Davis? He's not first tier?"

Carney refreshed his coffee with booze. "The old lady'd kill me if she knew I was doing this. Every time O'Gar, our publisher, sobers up, he goes to confession and then to Mass and then stalks through the second floor here and fires anybody he catches drinking on the job. That usually means me and a Jewish kid named Tom Fineman who thinks I'm pretty hot stuff so he imitates everything I do — including drinking on the job and getting fired whenever O'Gar thinks he's the Pope."

"But you're here now."

Carney nodded. "Yeah, as soon as O'Gar falls off the wagon, he comes to his senses and hires us back."

I laughed. "You've got a million stories."

"Yeah, I do. And like every journalist worth his salt, I suffer from the delusion that someday I'll write them up all nice and pretty in a book and make a lot of money and go fishin' the rest of my life." He had six hand-rolled cigarettes lined up along the edge of his desk. He stuck one of them in his mouth, ignited a lucifer with his thumb, inhaled, hacked, and said, "Arthur Davis fell out of favor with the first tier a few years back when he lost a very big case for one of the gentry here. It was a civil suit, a personal injury thing, and the rich gentleman was so guilty that not even Jesus could have convinced the jury that the man was innocent. So he doesn't go to any more parties."

"Serena Hopkins."

He shrugged. "She's fading a bit now, but she's one of the most sexual women I've ever seen. And a lot of men agree with me, judging from how many she's slept with. She married an older man for his money. There was a scandal and she ended up broke. She's been Arthur Davis's kept lady ever since, though I'm told they're not as close as they used to be."

Time to refresh his coffee again.

I wrote all this down in a kind of shorthand I'd developed in prison. The guards liked to tear up anything you wrote. And if you wrote anything personal and tender, they read it out loud and mocked you with it. They couldn't do that to me because they couldn't figure out what the shorthand meant.

"One more. Ted Nealon."

He smiled. "Ah, Ted. I doubt that's his real name and I doubt anything I told you about him would be helpful because it'd be mostly bullshit he tells about himself. He's a pretty boy with a very bad temper. I don't really know anything about him other than the fact that he has some connection to Larry Kimble. You see them together every once in a while. And that's strange because Larry Kimble is a very quiet, shy man who has decent instincts and acts on them most of the time. I get the impression Nealon would murder his own mother if the price was right."

He leaned back in his chair and *mooshed* his lips together and just watched me for a long minute. I tried not to be self-conscious. I looked right back at him.

"What I'm curious about, Mr. Mallory, is that you come here and say you're writing an article on the rich folks who pretty much run this whole part of the state. Or did I get that wrong?"

"No, you got it right."

"But the names you asked me about —

they aren't the powerful people. They're kind of the shady people, in some ways at least."

"That's why I wanted to check them out before I approached them."

He smiled. "You think I don't know when I'm being bullshitted? If you were really legit, you would've called the Chamber of Commerce or some organization like that and gotten the names of the families that run this city. And no matter who you talked to, the names you asked me about — Kimble and Davis and damned Ted Nealon — they wouldn't even have come up in the conversation."

"So your conclusion is what here, exactly?"

"Exactly? That you're probably a writer, all right. But that you're working some kind of local scandal that managed to elude me so far. Involving the folks you just named."

I laughed, relieved. He'd figured out that I was lying, but everything else he got wrong. Nothing involving Wally Tomkins, nothing involving queer money. "You're irritated because I'm working a story you haven't picked up on yet."

"I thought I knew everything that went on here." He picked up another cigarette.

Lighted it. "Maybe we could work it together," he said, winking at me when smoke got in his right eye.

"To be honest, I'd have to think about that." I stood up, pushed my hand out. "Thanks for your help. I really appreciate it. And I really will think about what you said."

I said good-bye and left.

Before going to introduce myself to Mr. Lawrence K. Kimble, I went back to my hotel to drop off the notes I'd taken at the newspaper and to pick up the money I'd need as my introduction to the esteemed Mr. Kimble's bank.

There was a woman several steps ahead of me on the stairs in my hotel. She wore a simple blue skirt and a simple white blouse. She carried several books cradled in her arm. She stumbled on the top step. She was able to stay upright, but the books flew from her arms to the floor.

I helped her pick them up. I didn't get a look at her face until I placed the last book in her arm. The simplicity of her skirt and blouse fit well with the simplicity of the chestnut-colored hair and the large, perfect brown eyes. She'd no doubt broken a lot of hearts, this one. Not because she was exotic or coy. She had the simple, freckled prettiness of the teacher you fall in love with when you're a little boy; or the quiet girl who never quite took to you because you were too noisy and full of yourself; or the married woman you see in a store one day and fall almost painfully in love with for an hour or so, dreaming of all the different things you might have done with your life if only she'd been included.

"Thank you very much," she said.

"My pleasure."

"Are you on this floor?"

"Yes, ma'am, and I'll just bet it was you who threw that loud party last night, wasn't it?"

"The one with the brass band?"

"That's the one."

She smiled, and that just made her all the more fetching. "I wish I could say that I was in a mood for a party like that."

She started walking down the corridor and I fell into step beside her.

"My name's Natalie Dennis."

"I'm Dev Mallory."

"Dev?"

"Devlin."

"I think I like Devlin better, actually."

"I'd be happy to change it, but that means that all the Devs I have set in gold and rubies would have to be changed. And that could get expensive."

"I can see where that would get to be a problem. Being rich seems to be an awful chore." Her dark eyes got winsome. "At least to hear the rich tell it. I read an article by a prince once and according to him it was just a burden being rich."

I looked at the books she'd taken from the library. "You must've checked out every Sir Walter Scott novel they had."

"It's silly, actually. I know that a world like that never existed — all the intrigue and romance and derring-do — but I can forget my own world for a while and live in a book."

We were at her door. "I'm a writer, too."

"Really? I've never met a writer before."

"Magazine articles, so far. Though I'm hoping to get to a book one of these days."

"That's the best life I can think of. Writing. I read a piece on Robert Louis Stevenson. How he travels so much and everything. He's such a fascinating man."

"Yes, he is."

She turned to her door and inserted a key she'd taken from the pocket of her skirt.

"I hope I see you again, Natalie."

71

She glanced back at me. Smiled. "I was about to say the very same thing."

While I waited for Lawrence K. Kimble to see me, I sat in my best suit, my best boots, and my best social face reading a flier that featured Kimble on the cover saying: "The poor don't need handouts; they simply need to be taught self-respect, self-reliance, and self-help. Giving them food, clothes, and shelter will just destroy them!"

HEAR THIS DYNAMIC SPEAKER AT THE FIRST CONGREGATIONAL CHURCH JUNE 18 — CHRISTIANS, BRING THE FAMILY!

On the other side of the flier was a photograph of this stalwart visionary. Kimble had the kind of bland good looks that mothers like. The long head with the dark hair and the regular features bespoke intelligence, probity, and sincerity. The trouble was those eyes. Not even the huge circus smile could do anything about those sad and nervous eyes. I wondered what his secret was; he had toted some awful truth on his back for many, many years.

I looked up into the bright, competent face of Kimble's matronly secretary, who sat at a desk right outside his office. She wore a frilly white blouse that climbed right up to her jawline. Her face was narrow and severe but when speaking of Kimble, the blue eyes showed real pleasure.

"I keep telling him he should run for governor."

"Self-respect, self-reliance, and self-help," I said. "I don't personally know any poor people, but I'm sure they appreciate hearing things like this."

She apparently didn't hear the sarcasm in my tone.

"Well, some of them I feel sorry for. And I'm sure Mr. Kimble does, too. But the way they live —" She actually shuddered. "I went with our church group down to where the Jews and the coloreds live." The primness came back. "Of course, to be fair, they're not any worse than the whites. I've never seen so many unwashed children in my life. In white neighborhoods, I mean. And they run around naked right out on the street!"

I had mixed feelings about people in poverty, which was a topic of much discussion in the West these days. The recession seemed to be sliding into a depression. More and more people were poor. I was sure that a modest share of them could find work if they looked harder. But most of them were doomed by economic circumstances they couldn't control. Talk of self-reliance wasn't anything you could eat for supper.

Kimble wasn't quite as oily as his "dynamic speaker" flier implied. He had a firm but not extravagant handshake; a courteous but not overdone smile; and a surprisingly quiet voice and manner. He must have kept his thunderous "self-reliance" self in the closet and put him on the way you would a costume for a play.

His office was modest. The wainscoting was good but not the best; the deep wine-red carpeting was plush but not dense; and the furnishings were dark and tasteful but not top-of-the-line.

When we'd both taken chairs, he said, "Sorry to have kept you waiting. We've got a bank examiner coming — routine, thank God, nothing worse — and I had to look over these figures and get them to our accounting department."

"I'm in no hurry. Anyway, it gave me a chance to look over your flier."

He blushed. The blood came up like water

rising. And he said, "G-God, I w-wish she wouldn't p-put those things out th-there. I've t-told her and t-told her."

We both sat there staring at each other. The sudden stutter was sad and comic at the same time. He was clearly flustered and embarrassed by it. I had the sense that this was the secret that made his eyes so despairing.

"S-sometimes, I stammer. Usually it j-just c-comes on without any w-warning. The funny thing is —" He paused. Angled his head back and took a deep breath. And said, as he tilted his head downward: "There. That should do it." He shook his head. "It's a darn curse. Had it all my life. The funny thing is, when I put that pastoral robe on and step up to the public — I'm a pretty good orator. And I've never stammered once. And I've probably lectured at least thirty times over the past three years. My wife's idea, actually. She saw this singer once who stammered when he talked. But when he sang, he never stammered at all. She kept saying that maybe I should try that with my stammering. So I finally did it. I just sort of pretended I was a pastor and that these were my robes and I got up there and I spoke perfectly."

"That's a very impressive story."

He looked embarrassed now, as if he'd revealed too much about himself. "Well, that's probably not why you're here today, Mr. Mallory. Excuse me for going on that way."

I took the envelope out of my suit coat pocket and laid it on his desk. Except for a small stack of papers and a framed photograph, his desk was clean. The frame was angled so that I couldn't see the photograph itself. I pushed the envelope toward him. "There's three thousand dollars in there. I'd like to open a draw account."

"Well, that's certainly the way for a banker to start an afternoon. We appreciate your business, Mr. Mallory."

"My pleasure."

"Are you moving here?"

"No. But I'll probably be here for a month or so." I gave him the magazine writer story.

"Well, now, a writer. That's something I've always thought I'd like to try if I ever had a little time. I mean, it's probably not as difficult as most people think. If they just applied themselves."

" 'Self-respect, self-reliance, and self-help,' just the way your flier says."

He chuckled. "Well, some people find

that a wee bit simple-minded, I realize. They think it's just a way of avoiding spending money on the poor. But I really believe that that's the only thing wrong with the so-called 'poor.' It's just gumption they lack."

I liked him better when he stuttered.

From the center drawer of his desk he took a large leather-bound volume. He checked to make sure that the carbon paper backing was in proper place, and then began filling out the form for opening an account. He asked me several more questions, and I answered them with all the usual lies.

"There's a window marked 'New Accounts' right inside the door, Mr. Mallory. If you'll take this form up there, they'll get you all set up so that you can start using your account whenever you'd like."

I stood up, leaning over slightly as I did so. I glanced at the photograph on the desk. It showed Kimble with the woman I assumed was his wife.

I'm not sure I can tell you exactly what I felt in the next thirty seconds — how to individually separate that turmoil of mixed feelings — shock, anger, grief, and a certain hard cold knowledge that I was about to see her again.

Her name was Cora back when I knew her. She was my wife and she'd run out on me without ever getting a divorce.

I was sure that if I told Lawrence K. Kimble all this, he'd start stammering again.

PART TWO
VINCENT ROBERT KELLY

So one time this copper said to Vincent Robert Kelly, "You should do something with your life, Vince. I get tired of arrestin' you. You're smart, you dress good, and you got enough charm and bullshit in ya to get yourself elected mayor."

At the time, and this was in Philadelphia, what Vince was doing involved prostitution. The slums were such that he could easily recruit young girls — he never dipped below age thirteen; he had standards, after all — washed them up, dressed them up, shined them up, and escorted them through the corridors of the finest hotels the city had to offer. This was his preferred method of operation. You didn't get as many sales as you did on the street, but you got paid much more and you dealt with a much higher class of gent, one unlikely to beat the girls (in such opulent settings, a young girl screaming was likely to attract attention) or quibble over the bill.

His second method of operation was working the taverns and saloons where poor workingmen drank. Paying off the beat cop was no problem, nor was stashing two or three girls (not of the caliber he brought to the hotels). He had a big Negro with him who made sure he didn't have any trouble with his customers. And so, one by one, two by two, three by three, the drunken workingmen would come out back, pay their money, and go into a cheapjack shed with two mattresses on the floor. Kelly always found all the grunting and groaning vulgar. He usually paid one of his runners to oversee the operation with the big Negro.

The third operation was what the law called panel thieving. This required some skill and the cooperation of a hotel. Needless to say, not a hotel on the level of his first operation, rather hotels run by sweaty, drunken men who could procure abortions, illicit drugs, girls or boys (your choice) and point you in the direction of cockfights, dog fights, and the latest craze called ratting — a dog is put in a cage with a dozen rats that have been starved for nearly a week. You watch as the rats rend and devour the dog. You bet on how long it will take for the rats to do their work.

The panel thieving required renting a room in which a false wall had been installed. Your gal brings her drunken customer to the room and proceeds to have sex with him while the panel is silently opened (you had to get the panel just right) and you steal the man's money and anything else in the clothes he's draped over the nearby chair. Then the panel is slid back. The drunk usually doesn't realize he's been robbed until he's back on the street. Or waking up in the morning with his wife screaming at him, "Where'd ya go last night, you besotten son of a bitch?"

It was the panel thieving that ultimately brought the smooth street crook Kelly down. One of his thieves had been indulging in cocaine and was none too steady. He slid the panel back all right and got to the chair all right. But then he fell over it.

Drunken lover leapt from the bed and proceeded to smash the thief's head in. And he did a damned good job of it. The drunken lover was a massively built steelworker and he intended to take no shit from some scrawny dope-taker who was trying to rob him. The seventeen-year-old died on the spot from several head injuries.

The drunken lover was found guilty of an infraction of law nobody, including the prosecuting attorney, had ever heard of before this trial. He got a bench parole.

The girl was let go, too.

Kelly was not so lucky. The prosecuting attorney was able to convince a jury that if Kelly wasn't the devil himself, he'd do till the real thing came along.

It was in prison that Kelly finally decided, as both his cop friend and reformers had begged him, to "do something with his life."

After convincing his rather large cellmate that it was nothing personal, that he, Kelly, was just uncomfortable with, again nothing personal, having any sort of intimate contact with a man — it was after they got that little matter taken care of . . . It was after that that Len the cellmate started telling nightly tales of his cousin Bobby who, Len claimed, ran a successful counterfeiting operation in Mexico and was planning someday to bring his skills across the border and soak the fucking *federales* for every greenback they were worth.

It would be sacrilegious to suggest that Kelly's conversion came to him in the form of a religious vision — the Lord wasn't likely to appear to a man and tell him about a nifty new method of breaking the law — but it was as close to a religious vision as the likes of Kelly would ever have.

He was going to forgo pimping, armed robbery, arson, rolling drunks, and stealing from the church poorbox on holy days. No more of that low-down, low-life criminality for him.

Over the next three years — leading the life of a model prisoner — he learned about the intricacies of counterfeiting . . . zinc plates and watermarking and paper weight and paper texture and inks and dyes and the dangers of smudging and fading.

He also told the warden that he'd decided against parole. He would serve the entire four years. He told the lawyer he wanted to get a job in Washington, D.C., where his cousin (actually a fake priest who helped sell nonexistent Bibles and burial plots to folks dumb enough to buy them) lived, certain that Father Delaney would be a good influence on him.

The warden grinned. "You've got more shit in you than a Christmas turkey, Kelly. But it's a damned good story. Damned good. Nobody's ever come up with that priest angle before." He shrugged. "You want to stay in here another year, fine by me. Just do me a favor."

"Sure, Warden."

"Every once in a while come up here and tell me one of your stories. You're really good, kid. In fact, I can't think of anybody better."

"Well, I appreciate that, sir."

Kelly heard the warden chuckling to himself as he left the office.

"My cousin's a priest," the warden said aloud. "I've got to tell my wife that one at dinner tonight. She'll love it."

Kelly's new calling was reconfirmed when, just after his release from prison, Vince was passing through Boston and saw an old friend of his, a key burglar named George Watson. Watson told Vince about a counterfeiting operation this gang had broken into in a basement printing operation where the operators appeared to be getting rich. And soon after, he met yet another old and mercenary friend — a man he'd always considered something of a mentor, one Mitch Michaels.

ONE

During the war, the Boss worked for the Secret Service. Few people seem to know, or care, that the Secret Service is in charge of investigating counterfeit money operations. During the war, on both sides, maybe as much as 50 percent of all paper currency was queer. This could have proved fatal to either side. And it wasn't just criminals who counterfeited money. Even countries did it. One way the Brits tried to defeat us during the American Revolution was to float so much bad money that our real currency was virtually worthless. Since then, other countries had tried as well.

The counterfeiting continued not only after the War Between the States began, but also even after 1862 when the first official national currency started rolling off the presses.

I spent most of the war setting up counterfeit schemes for a friend of mine named Phil Darcy, who was a sub-cabinet officer in the Lincoln administration. We'd been roommates at Dartmouth. We'd also spent seven months together on three different cattle drives, dropping out of college for a year so we could learn to be cowboys. We wanted to prove — mostly to ourselves — what manly young men we were. At the start, we gave the cowboys some pretty good laughs, I'm sure. But after a couple of months, we started catching on. We rode drag as they call it, and doubled our weight in dust alone. Try riding behind a couple hundred head of cattle sometime and you'll see what I mean. The dust gets so heavy you have to wear a bandanna the same way you have to in a sandstorm. I broke an arm getting thrown off a horse, two fingers when I got them caught in a rope, and still have a knot just above my ear from one of the many fistfights I'd gotten into. Cowboys seem to think that beating the shit out of each other is a good way to pass the time.

Then the war started. Phil's father was a good friend of Lincoln's. He swung the job for Phil and Phil enlisted me. The object was simple. Help Jefferson Davis run out of funds even faster than he was already. I passed a couple hundred thousand dollars of queer money before being found out and put into a prison where the Confederacy held those spies they had decided against hanging or shooting. They spared me and Wally Tomkins so we could help them figure out the patterns the Boss was using in spreading his counterfeit. About the time they realized we weren't all that much help, the war ended.

Wally came from farm folks and had no money. I came from money that had been lost through bad investments. We decided, Wally and I, in a larky sort of way, to start printing Union money and make our living as itinerant counterfeiters.

I met Cora Dane on a riverboat. She was the most bedazzling woman I'd ever seen. She was also bright, funny, and a world-class confidence woman, except for those times that she called her "gray" days when she could barely do anything except stay in bed and weep. Sometimes, she told me, this had to do with her monthly visitor and sometimes not. I'd slept with her several times but got the impression that our brief couplings meant a hell of a lot more to me than they did to her.

I didn't see her again until the early 1870s, when I was working as a Pinkerton. Washington was starting to pay severe attention to counterfeiting operations. They sent a couple of operatives to shut us down and/or kill us. I think they would have preferred the latter. I had a friend who was the number-five man at the Pinkertons. I explained my situation and said that if I promised the Secret Service to retire from counterfeiting, would they consider dropping charges against Wally and me. At that time Alan Pinkerton, who had been so successful running the spying operation in the war, could get pretty much what he wanted from Washington. Wally and I became Pinkerton agents.

A year into my new employment, I was given the assignment of finding out what this rich old man's lovely young wife was up to. The wife turned out to be Cora Dane. It was easy enough to tail her, easy enough to see what she was doing. There was a handsome young Frenchman, and they met several times a week in a servant's cottage on the old man's estate.

Now handsome young Frenchmen have one thing in common — they want it all. Take this one. While Cora was being dutiful to the withered old bastard who was pathetically in love with her — and who, I later found out, couldn't do anything about it in the sexual area — the Frenchman was keeping two other ladies happy. What the two other ladies had in common was that they were married, had once been but no longer were beautiful, and had at their disposal a great deal of money thanks to their indifferent husbands, who undoubtedly had much younger ladies on the side.

From these women our Frenchman got his walking-around money. They would use him in the suites they kept respectively in expensive hotels, pay him, and get rid of him for the day. The dread of full old age had made them tough and wise, and neither had any illusions about the very busy lad who brought them the kind of hard, sweaty sex of their youth. Hard and sweaty was fine for hotel boudoirs, but hardly for the parlor or café. . . .

The Frenchman had exotic tastes in entertainment. This was the year that ratting came into popularity in the city. He went three times a day to a huge barn along the river where men laid huge bets on the outcome of the gory battle. I've never forgotten the screams of the dogs right before the rats took to ripping off noses and hooking teeth into eyes. The Frenchman spent most of his money on the ratting. And almost invariably lost.

For a day or two there, I was afraid he'd become aware of me following him. He glimpsed me a couple of times. And once

89

he took off running. He wasn't aware of me finding him a few minutes later.

He seemed to see Cora increasingly during May. By then I was planning, literally, on killing him. Whatever stripe of whore she was, she shouldn't have been with some male prostitute whose pleasures included the death of sad and scared and innocent dogs. In fact, I hated him so much by this time that one night I waited outside a café where he was romancing yet another older woman. I put a bandanna around my face and lurked in an alley near where her coachman and hansom cab waited. I am a past master at lurking, as are most Pinkertons.

I made it look like a robbery. . . . I took her purse and ripped open his suit jacket with my pocketknife so that I could find his paper money. Then I worked on him. I broke his nose and his jaw and three of his fingers on his left hand. I just kept thinking of those dogs. I probably would have killed him if I hadn't heard a police whistle.

Cora and the Frenchman saw each other more and more often. She snuck down the back stairs and met him in the moonlit mansion's backyard. On the nights they made love in the gazebo, I had to walk away. The sounds they made made me as sick as the cries of the dogs. I didn't want him touching her. I wanted to cut his hand off with an ax.

I sensed this was all coming to an end, and it was.

One night I followed the Frenchman from his hotel to the old man's mansion. He didn't go to the gazebo that night. Instead, he slipped in a side door, which was ordinarily locked. I knew something was about to happen. And it did, a few minutes later, announced by two shots, small barks, which told me that the caliber of gun used was small.

I used the same side door the Frenchman had. Standing just inside, a door to my left leading to the basement, a door at the top of four steps in front of me, I pulled my Colt and listened for any further sounds. Somewhere, a grandfather clock chimed nine. And, more faintly, a fire crackled comfortably in a fireplace. Other than that, silence.

I went up the steps in front of me, ready for somebody to jerk the door open at any time and fire down on me. The Frenchman, of course. Escaping. I had a good notion of what I'd find eventually. Cora would say that a burglar had broken into the mansion and killed her husband.

The Frenchman would get away and when it was safe, they would meet and run away with the old man's fortune. A cliché, true, but it happens frequently to keep the penny newspapers in lots of lurid stories.

The kitchen was restaurant-big and restaurant-fancy. The dinner parties here were likely mythic, the stuff of society-page legend. The rest of the downstairs matched the kitchen in size and ambition. The furnishings ran French, delicately carved in contrast to the heavier British style just coming into vogue. Two rooms bore massive chandeliers, but the house was shadowy because only wall sconces were lighted. The fieldstone fireplace was big enough to hold a picnic in. An enormous black cat sat on a settee, great green eyes following me with fierce interest. He knew that somebody as common as me didn't belong here.

The grand staircase wound wide up into the darkness of the second floor. Somebody was moving around up there, footsteps faint. By now I was sweating hard and my breath was coming in uneven gasps. I guess even then I knew I would have to make a terrible decision very soon. What I wanted to do was figure out a way to separate Cora from the Frenchman, hang the old man's murder on him alone.

But how could I do that? He was weak. The police would have his whole story in a few hours. And they would love to push Cora's part in this. A beautiful woman, a handsome French lover, a dead old man and his millions — what cop, what reporter could resist that?

The staircase steps were carpeted, so I made very little noise. I had a nasty taste in my throat. A slashing headache was starting to divide my skull. I was thinking all sorts of ridiculous but tempting thoughts: Would there be a way to kill the Frenchman and make it look as if he'd killed the old man by himself? And then Cora'd been forced to kill him in self-defense? With the right lawyer, she'd at least have a chance. I could help her set it up. . . .

The hallway stretched east and west into gloom. It took me a moment to see the thin pale line of light beneath a door at the far end of the hall.

No voices. No sound. Just that frail edge of light that I moved toward knowing that whatever I found it wasn't going to be good. Going to the police made the most sense; going right back down the stairs and walking to find a copper and letting him take over the entire investigation.

I didn't, of course. Because Cora was

going to be grateful to me, so grateful that she'd do whatever I said, and whatever I said was going to involve us getting married.

I leaned my head to the door. A sound — something being dragged across the floor. A tiny female cough. Cora. The best way in is surprise. I put my hand to the doorknob, gave it a half twist, shoved the door inward.

She didn't see me in the doorway at first. She was in the process of dragging the Frenchman further away from the body of her husband. Over to the point where the small handgun lay on the Persian rug. So it would look as if they'd shot at each other and had died for their trouble.

While this particular story wasn't as common as the one where the lover shoots the husband and then hides until the time is right to appear again and join hands with the widow and her new fortune . . . this one made for a better story, at least for my purposes. Though it would take some getting used to. Killing her husband told me a few things about Cora I hadn't especially wanted to know. But this —

"Put his legs down, Cora. And then stand up straight with your arms in the air."

94

She didn't react as most people would have. Your average killer would have snapped her head up and stared at me with terror and anger. But she wasn't most people. She was Cora. She raised her head slowly and when she saw who I was, she smiled and said, "A gentleman would offer a lady some help in a situation like this. He's heavier than he looks."

"I'm serious about what I said, Cora. I'm arresting you."

In a certain way, it was ridiculous, of course. Here she stood holding up a dead man's legs and smiling at me in that slow soft way she did after we had made love. "I knew you'd find me again, someday. Believe it or not, I never forgot about you, either."

She eased the Frenchman's feet to the floor and stood up straight. She wore a dark green dressing gown that flattered the red hair and the green eyes and the wide, tawny mouth. Even given the heavy cotton, the shape of her couldn't be hidden. She saw me as my eyes paused on her breasts. Her smile grew more confident. "I really mean that, Dev. I really never have forgotten about you."

"Kept yourself pure for me, huh?"

"You're making fun of me, Dev, but you

shouldn't. There hasn't been a day go by that I haven't wondered if I made a mistake, running out on you that way."

"Or cheating on me. Or stealing from me. Those mistakes, too, Cora?"

She took a step toward me.

"The hands go up in the air, Cora. Just like I said."

She took another step toward me.

I reached into the left pocket of my suit coat and brought out a pair of handcuffs.

She said: "We could be together again, Dev."

"Just like the good old days, huh?"

"I mean it, Dev. I've changed."

I laughed harshly. I couldn't help it. "God, Cora, you're standing here with two dead men at your feet and you tell me you've changed? Now since you won't put your hands up, put them straight out in front of you."

For the first time, alarm showed in those soft sweet eyes of her. The handcuffs made it all real to her suddenly. "You're not serious about this, Dev. You can't be."

"The arms, Cora. Right out in front of you."

"What if I told you that François killed him?"

"And you killed François because you

96

were so outraged? Juries are pretty skeptical about things like that."

"I made a mistake. I had a small affair. I regretted it and told my husband. He forgave me. We planned a trip. London. London was my poor husband's favorite city and —" By the end of this little theatrical turn, even she couldn't take her words seriously. She was teasing me with it, making melodramatic fun of how an innocent widow would sound in the defendant's box.

I took two steps, grabbing her left wrist, bringing it up, clamping the cuff on. "And François here was so heartbroken that he came up here and demanded that your poor old husband let you go and —"

"— and they argued. And when I heard the shot, I ran upstairs and found Charles dead on the floor there. François grabbed me and pleaded with me to run away with him. And when I wouldn't, he threatened me with the gun and pressed it right to my heart and we struggled and —"

Then I got the second cuff on her.

"I can't believe this, Dev. You know you're still in love with me. You should see your face. You can hardly keep your hands off me. And I want you, too, Dev. I really do. When you came through the door there — I realized what a terrible mistake I'd made running out on you, stealing from you those times —"

The words drifted away as I walked around the den. Floor-to-ceiling leather-bound books on two walls, a huge window overlooking the grounds on the east window, and a framed map of the world on the west. Heavy leather-covered furnishings, framed art depicting various historical battles down the ages, and a subdued portrait of Cora that managed to make her look demure if not downright virginal.

I stood before the painting the way people did in a museum. I searched it for some hint of truth in the face. But the portrait artist had been good indeed. The only truth of it was that it was a fraud and that seemed to fit Cora better than I wanted it to.

I turned back to her. "How did it make you feel? Killing two people like that?"

"Oh, Dev, I don't deserve being treated like this. Like some — animal."

I did a stupid thing, then. I walked over to her. To that wonderful body I'd known so well. To that dark and cunning and ingenious mind. I suppose she knew by then that I couldn't go through with it. I hadn't realized that yet. I still had a few more self-righteous little speeches to give. And I gave them. And all the time I did, the scent of her, the flesh of her, that candlelight-soft gray gaze of hers — I was suffused with her then. Every molecule of mine interspersed with every molecule of hers. I could barely swallow or breathe.

She knew not to smile. Or to make an overt advance. She sensed that sex would be the wrong thing to offer me at this moment, that it would only confirm my suspicions. She said softly, "That night I said you'd make a good father? Do you remember that, Dev? And then I said you'd make a good husband, too? Do you remember that, Dev? I'd never said anything like that to a man. Not ever. Doesn't that mean anything to you, Dev? Don't you remember that night?"

I kissed her. I couldn't stop from kissing her. And after a time, she laughed quietly and said, "I think this would work much better if I didn't have handcuffs on."

And my voice — all the hard harsh purpose of it was gone. I was her lover again. "I suppose you want me to take them off. . . ."

"I guess the thought *had* crossed my mind, Dev."

And even worse, as I was unlocking the cuffs, I heard myself say, "That story of yours needs a lot of work."

"Will you help me with it?"

Sometimes the law is lenient on a person charged with accessory to murder. A father helping a son; a wife helping a husband — they get little if any prison time even if their loved one is convicted of first-degree. But a man who helped a beautiful adulteress cover up a double homicide? The law would show no mercy.

"Men have affairs and aren't found guilty. I can just say that I'd made a mistake. And that my husband forgave me. And François became insane —"

"Men are allowed to have affairs — not women. Women who have affairs are whores. In the minds of jurors. Juries convict whores."

She looked at me and said. "Is that what *you* think of me, Dev, that I'm a whore?"

I took the whiskey she gave me and said, "I think you killed two men in cold blood. And now I think you're a woman in very deep trouble. You got the killing part down. But you didn't think the aftermath through very well." I touched her cheek. The sensation made me dizzy. All these years I'd waited to be alone with her. And now it had to go and be like this. "Your beauty isn't going to help you at the trial, Cora. In fact, it's going to hurt you. The

100

women will resent you and the men'll think about sleeping with you — but they'll resent you, too. You're the kind of beautiful woman they've dreamed about all their lives but were never able to have. They'll pay you back for being so unreachable. They'll vote to hang you." I nodded to her dead lover sprawled on the floor. "There's one thing in our favor. Frenchie here." I nodded to François on the floor. "His name wasn't François, by the way. It was David Janvier and he was wanted for two murders in Paris. Did he ever bother to tell you that?"

She looked right at me and laughed. It was a merry laugh, considering the two dead men in the room. "No, but there were a number of things I didn't bother to tell him, either."

Then she took my hand and touched it to her cheek again. Every part of my body responded. She must have felt something, too, because her eyelids fluttered shut as in a moment of great wild pleasure.

And then she smiled and said: "You never forgot me, did you?"

And then I smiled, too, and damned myself for saying. "I tried hard to forget you, Cora. I tried *very* hard."

If you're looking for the start of it, the

exact moment when we knew that we were going to work together to keep her from the gallows, there it was. Right there and right then, it was.

We didn't get the police for more than an hour. She wasn't bothered by using their wedding bed, but I forced her to go a little further down the hall to one of the guest rooms. Sleeping in a dead man's bed would have been like sleeping in a coffin.

I put a number of bruises on her arms, back, and thighs before the police arrived. This was to demonstrate that her husband beat her constantly. She had the idea for the broken nose. It was such a fine and elegant nose that I almost couldn't do it. I broke it as clean as I could. As it turned out, the slight break right at the top only added to the majesty of that face.

I testified at the inquest and that was all it took. The district attorney, much against his will, listened to the cooler heads of his staff and decided not to bring charges against Cora. I was an honorable Pinkerton. I testified that I'd seen Frenchman David Janvier skulk into the house. I said that I followed him in, worried that he'd looked crazed. Moments later, I said, I heard two gunshots. Janvier had been hit first in the chest, but had had time to shoot the old man in the forehead. Just as I burst through the door of the den, I saw them both falling to the floor. I also pointed out that he was wanted for two murders in Paris.

A month later, Cora and I were married in New Orleans. We had a three-day honeymoon and then I went back to work. I took her with me, asking for longer assignments so that we could stay in a place two or three months instead of always being en route to somewhere. Sex became a drug for me. I kept the taste of her juices in my mouth, savoring them, whenever I had to be away from her for any time. My hands literally ached for the touch of her.

I suppose there were others before the drummer. Eight months into our marriage, on a day when I was supposed to be checking out a crooked accountant, I got back early and found them in bed in our hotel room. You hear a lot of jokes about such situations. The humor is usually about the violence that follows a man catching his wife in bed like this.

The funny thing is, in memory anyway, it was all pantomime. Not a single word was spoken. The kid, and that's what he was, no more than seventeen or eighteen, got up and pulled on his shirt and pants and shoes, nodded to Cora, and left. She stayed in bed, the covers pulled modestly up over her breasts.

There was a bottle on the bureau. I went over and poured myself a shot. I picked up the framed photograph of us on our wedding day, smashed frame and glass, and then tore the picture in half and dropped it in the wastebasket.

I went out without a word. The next time I saw her she was bailing me out of the lockup — and believe me, Inquisition torturers had nothing on the guards in that city jail — where I'd been for the past nine hours on the charge of drunk and disorderly. Not only did I have to pay for the saloon I'd smashed up. There was going to be a dental bill for the two men whose teeth I'd knocked out. I didn't even have the pleasure of remembering any of this.

After that, if we spoke, it wasn't much. At least it's that way in memory. We used words only when necessary. I slept on the floor next to the bed. I'd never really seen her humbled before except for those times when her so-called "miseries" came, the staying in bed. The weeping. She wasn't the humble sort. But this was real misery more than humility. She appeared to be as baffled by what she'd done as I was. I saw her writing letters to me. One night she started crying as she wrote and then tore up the letter in fury. I never did get to see any of those letters.

It was two months before we made love again. I had a Dartmouth friend who told me that he knew this town girl he'd been seeing had been unfaithful to him because when he slipped into her, her vagina was cold. I told him he was imagining things. But then I must have had a similar imagination because the first few times we had sex following the incident with the kid, I swore her vagina was oddly cool.

The worst of it was when she got pregnant and then miscarried. I'd been wondering if the child was mine, anyway. That's maybe the worst kind of self-doubt of all. To make things worse, she drank poison while I was gone — the miscarriage had devastated her — and was saved only because a doctor happened to be in the neighborhood.

Soon after, I had a case involving a large stash of diamonds that would be delivered by train. The merchant and I were the only two who knew the schedule other than the man transporting them. I came back to our room one night and saw that my report, where I kept running notes of my work, had been gone through carefully. Or certain pages of it, anyway.

The next morning, I met the courier at the train. We climbed into a hansom cab and headed for the jeweler's. Or I thought we did, anyway. The driver took us inside a huge, dark barn on the eastern edge of town. Two masked people in black shirts and Levi's came out of the dank gloom of the barn. They both toted shotguns. Easy enough to recognize Cora and a man named Vince Kelly. He'd always been on the edges of her life, but she'd been adamant that they'd never been lovers. When the courier didn't hand the diamonds over immediately, Kelly shot him twice in the face. He was dead before he was able to slump to the ground.

Then he walked over to me. I had no doubt he'd shoot me, so I handed over the black leather case with all the diamonds. When he had them, he tossed them to Cora. Then he smashed my nose with the butt of his shotgun. Then he threw me out of the cab.

Cora and Kelly climbed inside. Their driver lashed the horses and they raced from the barn at full tilt.

I was lucky the Pinkertons hadn't pressed charges against me. But they believed me that I'd had nothing to do with the robbery. By that time the Secret Service needed new agents to work on the counterfeiting operations out West. I was hired.

And then today, after all this time, I saw her in the photograph with Lawrence K. Kimble. His wife and mine.

TWO

I spent the next few hours going back through Wally's report. Not that I was getting much done. Cora kept haunting my room. A couple of times I believe I even spoke to her out loud. She didn't speak back.

Somewhere, sometime, I'd gotten the impression that she didn't matter to me one way or the other, that she'd hurt my pride more than anything else, and that she'd in all likelihood be in prison or the grave by now anyway.

But now I knew better. There's not a word that mixes hatred and love. You wouldn't think the human soul could balance two such feelings with equal ferocity, but it can.

Sitting there in the waning light of the day, the clamor and clatter of Denver's busy streets somehow distant now, I worked my slow and pathetic way through Wally's notes a paragraph at a time — and then surrendered to my thoughts of Cora.

Cora in bed with her teen lover. Cora sobbing after her miscarriage (our miscarriage, that's how it'd felt to me; *our* miscarriage). Cora and the diamond robbery.

Rage, pity, and a kind of awe. Her beauty, so regal and yet so fragile at times, made many of the things she'd done in her life unimaginable.

But that was Cora. Unimaginable.

Sleep came mercifully just a few minutes after I lay down. I dreamed of being a boy again, back East in the summertime, brushing my horse in the dusty hot sunlight and hearing my mother and father arguing on the large side porch. The subject was usually the same, the women my father saw whenever he took the train into New York. I had a school friend who said that when his parents argued, he'd just pick up a book and read and block the whole thing out. But I never could. Their shouts and curses ripped through me and left me shaking. I would be vaguely nauseous for the rest of the day. I could never get used to their shouting and cursing at each other. Even after all these years, I still had nightmares about their arguments, and would wake up shaky and sweaty.

Maybe I never got over their arguments because Cora and I had had the same kind of arguments ourselves. . . .

I slept for an hour before the knock came. I automatically slipped my gun into my hand and came up off the bed. "Who is it?"

"Natalie Dennis. From next door."

I brushed my hair with my fingers and took a quick shot of bourbon for any lingering sleep-breath. Then I went to the door and let her in.

She was still as pretty as a sentimental drawing of the girl you left behind. The enormous brown eyes made looking away impossible and the small nervous smile made her all the more endearing. I'd had coffee with her downstairs. She seemed to be as interested in me as I was about her. Though I wasn't sure if it was me or The Writer.

"I'm having my meal downstairs in an hour, Dev. I just thought maybe you'd like to join me."

"I'd like to. But I have to meet somebody else, I'm afraid."

Was that a flicker of pain in those eyes? I'd sensed a great sensitivity about her — one verging on a sorrow ready to ignite at any time — but I hadn't seen it quite this stark before.

"But tomorrow night would be fine," I said.

She made a show of looking happy. "Then tomorrow night it is."

She glanced beyond me to my room. The bed was unmade, there were clothes draped everywhere, the air was tangy with sleep and whiskey smells.

"Well, I just thought I'd ask."

She started to turn, but I took her slender wrist.

"How's it going with your father's attorney?"

She'd told me earlier that she was in Denver to straighten out some inheritance problems. She and her brother had become wealthy upon the death of their father a year ago. But the younger Tim was beholden to the bottle and reckless with money. He was also starting to amass a police record for alcohol-related crimes. She was here to see their lawyer and see if he could help.

"Well, I'm beginning to wonder if he isn't secretly working for my brother. He keeps telling me that I should settle. Just give Tim half of everything. But the trouble with that is he'll just squander it. The way he has all the other money Father gave him. I wanted to set up some kind of trust for Tim. He's twenty-one, but I'd have it so that the fund doesn't start giving him any money until he takes the cure."

"The 'cure'?"

"There's a hotel just outside of Denver here. It offers a program for weaning people off alcohol or drugs. I told the attorney that I'd be willing to give Tim five thousand dollars if he finished the program. It's seven weeks without alcohol of any kind. He said he'd speak to Tim's lawyer."

"What're the chances of Tim doing something like that?"

"Not very good." She sighed, knotted her small hands together. Made a worried face. No matter how she distorted her looks, she couldn't alter its basic prettiness. "It's his friends as much as the liquor. They get into a lot of trouble. But since they all come from prominent families, they're usually able to get out of it. Some family member is a good friend of the presiding judge or something like that. Most of the time. But he's still got a fairly extensive police record."

"Maybe a little jail time would bring Tim around."

"Oh, no." And she pressed a hand to her breasts. "Tim couldn't handle jail. He likes to pretend that he's tough but he's not. The alcohol — he's very prone to forgetting these days — he's so weak these days. Like a little boy." She shook her head. "Alcohol is such an insidious poison. You should hear him when he has nightmares. The way he screams. You'd swear somebody was trying to kill him. I always rush into his room and hold him the way you would a little boy. It always takes me a while to get him calmed down, to make him see that the monsters he says are chasing him are all in his head. It's so sad — there's so much potential in him."

"Maybe he's at the point where he'll listen. Maybe he'll give that program a try."

"I hope you're right, even though I'm skeptical." As she said this, she looked at me carefully. "Is everything all right?"

"A little tired is all."

"That must be it." She gently poked my arm. "The sparkle's gone from your eyes."

"I'll buff up my baby blues tonight. By tomorrow, they'll be sparkling the way they usually do."

"You've had to listen to my troubles, Dev. I'll be happy to listen to yours."

"I appreciate you saying that, but I'll be fine."

She lingered. "If you're sure."

I surprised both of us by leaning over

and kissing her on the cheek. She inhaled sharply and a blush came to her face. "I'll be fit company by this time tomorrow night. I promise," I said.

I rented a horse and saddle from the livery. The first place I stopped was Wally's old apartment.

Nan Julian, the quietly pretty redhead, was scrubbing down the front porch with a mop and bucket. Most places knocked money off your rent if you chipped in. She paused as I reached the front steps, wiping forehead sweat away with a sleeve of her cheap blue shirt. She looked awfully damned good in her jeans.

When she saw me, she said, "You ready for a cup of coffee because I sure am?"

"That doesn't sound bad at all."

Mop went into bucket, girl went into house. She was back in a few minutes bearing two steaming mugs of coffee. We sat on the front steps waiting for our coffees to cool and watching the show a couple of worm-hungry jays were putting on for us in the grass. It was a clear, summer-cool morning. Even the air smelled good.

"I'm pretty sure you didn't come to see me," she said. "So it must be about Wally."

She said this in a flirty, good-natured

way, but I was surprised that she was interested in me at all. I was older, the face that had once been almost pretty was now battered; even though I was slim there was the start of a little belly, and the dark hair was shot with gray. She should be out dancing with young fellas when the moon was full and the fiddles at their merriest, not sitting on a front porch with the likes of me.

"You know, it's possible I came here for both reasons. To see you *and* to talk about Wally."

"Very good, Mr. Mallory. An answer like that, you could be a politician."

"Just what I've always wanted to be."

She blew on her coffee. "So let's talk about Wally. In fact, I had a dream about him last night. He was walking down this long, dark corridor. I kept hollering for him to come back. To not go any further. But he wasn't listening. Or he couldn't hear. He didn't stop, anyway. He just kept going further and further down this long dark hall —" She tentatively sipped her coffee. "I really got close to him. He was like my uncle Gus. Gus just died last year. There wasn't anything I couldn't talk about with Uncle Gus. And Wally was like that." She shrugged. "I like older men. I've never been able to figure out why. But men my age — they just don't have enough experience on them to be interesting."

An ice wagon came clattering past. At least half-a-dozen dogs came flying out of nowhere. The morning's theatrical show had come at last. The ice truck with a spavined old horse.

"Did many people come to see Wally?"

She thought about it. "No, not really. In fact, I can only think of one in all the time he was here."

"Do you remember who that was?"

"Oh, sure. Hard to forget. This really beautiful woman. This hansom cab pulled up and there she was. She had this really expensive suit on — the kind fancy ladies always wear in magazines — and she went up the side stairs to Wally's apartment. I got busy with laundry and things so I wasn't around when she left. I'm not even sure how long she was up there."

"Wally ever mention anything about her?"

"No. And that was funny, too. I fixed dinner for us a lot and he usually told me how his day went and everything. I never could figure out what he did exactly — I got the sense he didn't want me to know — but he'd tell me that he went here and there, things he'd seen and places he'd been, things like that. You know how people talk over dinner."

"This woman? Could you describe her?"

No mistaking who she was telling me about. Cora.

"He mention her to you? Wally, I mean?"

"That was the funny thing. He didn't. I finally kind've teased him about it. He just mumbled something about somebody he knew from the past. He obviously didn't want to talk about her."

"She ever come around again?"

"Not that I know of. And Wally sure wasn't going to mention her."

I finished my coffee. "You make fine coffee."

"Wally always said I was a good cook. You could always come to supper. Just give me a little bit of a warning so I can make something special."

I patted her on her denimed knee. "I just might take you up on that sometime. Thanks for the coffee and the talk."

From there I rode out to the Kimble estate on the southwest edge of the city. I was armed with my Colt and a pair of field glasses. I wasn't sure what good either of them would do me.

In the middle of maybe two acres sat a

large, two-story Georgian-style house with a dirt drive that swept up wide and long to the front steps. Several small fir trees kept the long front windows away from the eyes of people passing by on the road. I suppose it wasn't what you'd call a "first tier" mansion, but it would do till the real thing came along.

There was a woods behind the house. I decided that was the best place to do my spying from. The hardwoods formed a semicircle around the house. I took the horse back down the dusty main road until I found a place in the woods that looked to be a good entry point.

I tied the horse to a pine and started in.

When I was young, I liked to scare the hell out of myself by reading the Grimm Brothers. Nobody could describe haunted forests the way they could. The strange, glowing eyes that followed you from the dank off-trail shadows. The odd, choked cries of creatures that might well be satanic. The trails that led to massive, grotesque trees in which lived hopping little wizards and spell-casters, all eager to claim your body and eternal soul. Even the moonlight had an eerie cast to it, the moon of some alien world whose light distorted everything at least slightly.

I wanted to be scared that way again. Easy enough to dispel the terrible magic of the Brothers Grimm in the light of day. Forests weren't like that, especially in daylight. Forests were loamy places with sweet vulnerable little animals who would be some predator's meal. Forests were bramble and undergrowth, creeks no bigger than a trickle, fallen trees and the stiff hides and cracked bones of a thousand dead creatures. The closest most real forests came to the Grimm Brothers was when you saw a dog or a cat or a raccoon that was freshly dead, and you saw all the other creatures, including the maggots, feasting on it. That always gave you a moment's pause, wondering if nature would be any kinder to you when your time came.

I stood in the woods for well over an hour, putting the field glasses down only when I needed to go back into the woods and relieve myself. Then I was back in place, the field glasses to my eyes.

I just wanted to see her. I tried to convince myself that I'd come here for other reasons, but why bullshit yourself? I suppose I was interested in how Kimble lived. He was doubtless the leader of the counterfeit operation. His bank would be a perfect cover. I wanted to see her. She'd looked somewhat older than when I'd last seen her four years ago. But then that might just have been the photograph on Kimble's desk. All she had to do was come to one of the many windows available to her and stand there long enough for me to get a good sense of her appearance.

She appeared at the east end of the second floor. Just stood there, looking out, looking in my exact direction, in fact. Could she see me? I doubted it. But I could see her. She had aged some. The facial bones weren't as sharp, and the cheeks were fleshy and the chin padded. She wore riding pants of tanned leather and an emerald green tunic.

She would always be for me that mythical woman men carry around in their hearts like a lock of hair from their first failed love. A siren of patchwork shadows that revealed only parts of herself, the mysterious woman you are forever glimpsing in the windows of trains or restaurants or expensive hat shops. Glimpsed but never anything more. But they were glimpses that stayed with you for long years and remained more vivid in memory than most women you'd been intimate with. A terrible sense of loss came over me as I stood there watching her in that window, thinking of what might have been, what could have been, what should have been, but now could never be.

I wanted to kill her. I want to kill myself. I hated my weakness. I didn't want to be dragged through it all again. I knew I didn't have the strength to resist her, so my only hope was getting rid of her. But of course I wouldn't. I hated her and loved her too much for that.

When I first heard the faint rustling noise, I thought it was just some animal making its way through the underbrush. I'd probably counted twenty raccoons following this path tonight.

But the rustling got louder. It moved in my direction.

It took me a few more minutes to realize that the intruder was human. He was on the same path I'd taken. His tramping feet and weaving body announced his arrival well in advance.

I slipped into the deep gloom of the hardwoods that lined both sides of the path. I crouched down, laid my field glasses in underbrush so a stray moonbeam wouldn't catch on the lenses.

I didn't see his face. All I knew was that he was a big man in a dark suit and a dark fedora. He stood where I had for a few minutes. For a time, his breathing was the loudest noise in the woods. After a few minutes he walked up to the edge of the woods and waved.

I carefully angled myself so that I could see the window where she'd been. The window was empty now.

The silver glinted in the fractured moonlight on the trail. A hammered silver flask. He took a deep drink, started to cap the flask, and then decided on one more drink. This drink was double deep. His upper body convulsed when the spirits reached his stomach. Then he gave a long and satisfied sigh.

Then she was walking across the grounds in the back of the mansion, taking her time, carrying the sort of small cage people use to trap animals that might become pets. She wore a voluminous black dress so unfashionable it made me smile. Maybe Kimble didn't want her displaying her wares.

I wondered how many men she'd met in this way, sneaking out when the man she was living with fell asleep. She liked thrills and this had to be thrilling, the danger of it especially.

He started walking back down the trail, then stopped when it was impossible to see him from anywhere in the mansion. I got a good look at him. He wasn't wearing a mask tonight, as he had been the last time I'd seen him when he and Cora had stolen the diamonds and killed the courier. Vince Kelly.

I forced myself to think about the implications of Kelly being here. He was a Black Irisher with a temper that was as famous as his ways with the ladies. He was no doubt involved in the counterfeiting scheme. Kidnapping Henry Cummings may even have been his idea. Stealing the man who could steal legitimate plates — or make more if necessary — was a brilliant idea. And as much as I hated him, I knew Kelly was a smooth package.

They did everything they could with their clothes on. Then they started whispering. For the first time I pulled back from the moment and wondered objectively what they were talking about now. The warm whispers of lovers or the cold calculations of confidence artists?

Their parting scene was out of a stage play. Both waved archly to each other. I half-expected both of them to sob on cue.

I could almost feel her. Memories of touch, scent, taste came back to me along with that sense of icy dread that used to fill my gut when I knew she was hiding something from me. She could seem so simple and earnest and straightforward in a romantic moment, but then later on you'd begin puzzling through something she'd said or not said, and you'd know that she was never simple and earnest and straightforward — except at the sad time when she'd lost the baby and tried to kill herself.

Kelly turned back to the deepest woods, his horse no doubt being somewhere around here. Kelly cinched his hat on at a properly rakish angle, chuckling to himself in baritone satisfaction. The arrogance in the sound made me think of Lawrence Kimble and his stutter. Kimble was no match for Kelly, not in any sense. I felt sorry for him. Kelly would never let Cora get to him the way she'd gotten to Kimble and me.

The temptation was to come up from behind him, grab him around the throat, and smash his head into the nearest available tree. It was damned hard to resist.

But first I wanted to talk to Cora. Find out what was going on and just how deep she was in.

THREE

I was leaving my hotel room the next morning when Natalie Dennis came strolling down the hall and said, "I hope you haven't forgotten about our dinner engagement."

"I was just going out to buy you some rubies now."

She laughed. "You really are a writer. You always say exactly the right thing."

She was flower-fresh this morning, her sweet, wan face igniting into pure girlish pleasure when she laughed. "I just came back from breakfast downstairs. It was very good."

"I might try a little of that myself." It wasn't quite seven o'clock. I was hungry. I'd slept well. That always gives me an appetite.

"Well, see you tonight."

She touched my arm the way she had yesterday. It had the same effect on me as before. It put me in mind of all those schoolboy crushes I'd had in the summers when I'd come home from the private school my parents insisted I attend.

The hotel restaurant was crowded with drummers and local businessmen. Tobacco smoke mixed with griddle smoke made for a powerful odor, but by the time I was halfway through my first cup of coffee, I'd gotten used to it. I sat at a small table next to the window. Denver was coming to life, all that energy, success, and promise there to see in the way people hurried along the sidewalks, purposeful, singular. It was really a fine city.

The first time I heard the name "Davis," I didn't pay any special attention. Two heavily mustached businessmen sitting at a nearby table were lamenting the passing of a "Davis."

Then one of them said: "That damned Arthur, just think of all the secrets he took to his grave. He could have ruined half the important people in this town if he'd wanted to. And you know, I kinda thought he would. After he lost that case, I mean, and none of the rich people wanted him around anymore."

I put it together then. Arthur Davis. The attorney the newspaperman Jay Carney had told me about. The attorney Wally Tomkins had listed in his report as one of the men in the counterfeiting conspiracy.

126

I leaned toward the men and said, "Excuse me. I heard you mention Arthur Davis. Is that Arthur K. Davis?"

The thin man spoke. "Why, yes."

"He's the man I came here to see."

Thin man glanced at heavy man. Thin man said, "Well, I'm afraid it's bad news for you, then. He was found dead in his garden last night. Apparently, he'd tripped over something and smashed his head on a rock. But I'm sure somebody at his office will be able to help you. Poor old Arthur. A lot of people didn't like him. But he saw my father through some rough times back in the recession after the war. And never collected anything from him until my old man was solvent again. You don't forget a man like that."

"No, you don't. Thanks for the information."

The man nodded and went back to talking with his friend.

I suppose my first thought was one of coincidence, something too many people automatically rule out when considering deaths. They look for causes, foul play, heart seizure, alcohol. But damned strange things happen, things so strange that they're almost funny. A man in Baltimore once stepped on a rake. The handle hit

127

him square in the face and knocked him over backward into a small pond he'd built, his head cracking on a small marble swan, which, in turn, caused his upper body to fall in the water, which, in turn, ended up drowning him. The widow suspected foul play, but with the help of two open-minded young doctors from the medical school there, the Pinks were able to put everything in sequence through studying the various abrasions and cuts — forehead bruise and cut; broken nose; hair and brain matter on swan; angle of body; head hitting water; pond water in lungs. Not everybody believed this, of course, but nobody pushed for foul play anymore, either.

So I didn't find it difficult to believe that "poor old Arthur," as the man across the aisle called him, had succumbed to falling on a crack and contusing himself to death.

Cora didn't show herself till nearly noon, at which time I'd been hiding on horseback in the woods for nearly two hours.

These were different woods from yesterday's. These were on the east side of the road leading from the Kimble estate into town.

The day was bright, summery except for the mild temperature in the low eighties. I didn't intend on showing myself if she had company along. But it turned out she was alone in the shiny new black buggy with shiny red wheels.

I let her get a hundred yards past me on the road, and then I eased my horse into sight and started after her.

She must have been deep in her thoughts because she didn't seem to hear me until I was only a few feet from her buggy. Then she looked at me, looked away, and looked quickly back, as if just now recognizing me. She looked cute doing it, too. There was a moment of confusion while she debated which tack to take. Give her horse the whip and try and outrun me. Or pull to a stop and let me come alongside her. But she was a bright and sensible woman. She pulled over and let me come alongside her.

You always wonder how you'll meet your lost love someday. In reality, you probably never will see her again. Time and distance make it impossible. But still, you have these little dramas in your head. You meet again and she sees how wrong she was to leave you. That sort of thing. But if you do run into her somewhere sometime, it'll probably be in a mundane circumstance that leads to disappointment. By that time you're old and bald; or she's fat and has somehow grown a mustache.

I was neither old nor bald and she was certainly neither fat nor mustache-laden. But just at the point our eyes met, her horse began to unload a stream of smoking green-brown diarrhealike bowels that sure did spoil any possible romantic mood.

"I've never seen her do that before," Cora said, those eyes smiling and that wide, erotic mouth tugging into a grin. "I'm not sure that's a good omen, Dev."

I got down from my horse, led him to the side of the road, ground-tied him. "Pull your buggy over. There's a boulder over there we can sit on."

"What if I say no?"

I shrugged. Shook my head. "I know about Henry Cummings, Cora. I also know you're seeing Kelly on the sly. I'm also beginning to see the outline of the whole thing. You and Kelly use your husband to set up the money flow into various banks and systems and then when you get as much as you want, you and Kelly take off. It might even be that you kill him. He looks naïve enough to stand still for it, anyway."

She stared at me. She'd clearly been rocked by what I said. Twice she gave tiny gasps and made faces. I assumed her silence meant that she was trying to think of something that would rock me in turn. She'd be dramatic as always. I had to get my gasp mechanism ready. She always appreciated dramatic responses.

She said, "I'm going to have a baby, Dev."

She always enjoyed surprising people. Kept them off balance. Kept her in control. But usually, the tactic was to intimidate or belittle you in some way.

But when that wide, gorgeous smile broke across her face, I saw that rarest of emotions in her eyes, pure innocent happiness. "In a few days, in fact." She smoothed the voluminous blue dress — the mate to the black one she'd worn yesterday — to her belly. "It's like when I was pregnant with our baby, Dev. I don't show that much." Then she laughed. "You think this is a con?" She reached out and took my arm, bringing my hand to the belly I couldn't see all that well beneath the silk. But it was there, same as it had been the time she was pregnant with me, not very big, but I could feel the kicking.

"Isn't it wonderful?" she said.

My hand was still on her belly. The baby

131

kicked a few times. "He'll be just as ornery as you are, Dev."

"You figured out who the father is?"

Sometimes you say something so ugly you want to stop in mid-sentence. I hadn't even been aware of forming that thought. But there it was, in all its nasty glory.

She flung my hand away. "Thank you so much, Dev. I tell you about my baby and you insult me."

"I'm sorry."

"Sure you are, you sonofabitch." Her voice was raw with tears. "Just because I've made a few mistakes in my life." She shook her head.

I didn't push it, even though her "mistakes" included numerous long cons, bank robberies, and at least one murder. She had this sense of herself as an innocent victim. She seemed to believe that she wouldn't have done any of her terrible things if she hadn't been pushed into it by circumstance.

She turned, facing the road, picking up the reins. "I'm going into town now, Dev. Please stand back. And for what it's worth, Kelly turned up here a year ago and blackmailed my husband into going along with this. He said he'd turn me over to the law if Larry didn't cooperate. He was with this other man, this Mitch Michaels. I think Michaels was the leader. He was a lot smarter than Kelly. Anyway, Kelly starts forcing me to come out and meet him in the woods. He tells me he's still in love with me. He wants me to run away after we find the plates. He always forces me to kiss him. I go along with him because if I don't, he says he'll tell Larry some things that'll really turn Larry against me. Nothing illegal but pretty dirty stuff. I've had my moments, I have to admit that. What's funny is that I didn't realize I loved Larry until Kelly started manhandling me. I told him I loved Larry and when I heard myself say it, I realized that I meant it. I'm glad I married him. I want to spend the rest of my life with him."

I said, "He actually seems like a decent man, this time, Cora. Larry does. A lot better-quality man than I am. Or Kelly. I'm sorry you got blackmailed into this."

"Things were going so well before Kelly showed up." The pregnancy explained the puffiness of the face. It didn't explain the trace of fear that came into her eyes. "Somebody's killing us off — every one of us involved in this counterfeiting scheme. We can't turn to the law or even the Pinks. We just have to be very careful."

"You have any guesses as to who it is?"

Fear turned into anger. "One of us who isn't dead yet. We haven't been able to find Cummings or the plates. Larry bought a house on the edge of town and put Cummings in there. Then one day, he stopped by there to see how things were going and the house was empty. Cummings was gone and so was the printing press and all the paper — and the plates. Everybody's scrambling to find the plates. And Cummings. And now somebody's killing us on top of it."

"Arthur Davis died last night."

It was my turn to shock her, though I hadn't wanted to especially. She was desperate enough. I knew how much she wanted this baby. She didn't need to be scared any more than she was already.

"What happened to him?"

I told her.

"It wasn't any accident."

"I don't think it was, either."

My hand idly touched hers. I said, "Ouch." I was only half-joking.

"Hot, huh?" She laughed. "I'm just running a little fever, the closer we get, I mean. I'm sure it's not serious."

"You talk to a doc?"

"Dev, if I believed everything a doc ever

told me, I would've been dead a long time ago. I'm using a midwife. I've got a lot more faith in them. Larry made me go to his doc a couple of times, but I didn't like him at all. I think the only reason he wanted to see me was so he could get my clothes off. And I'm serious."

She'd always been like that. Hated docs, I think because they frequently gave her bad news. So when she needed medical help, she tended to go to people who were one step up from quacks or con artists. At least midwives were usually professional at their calling.

"Listen to me, Cora. I can help you. I can't give you any details but if you'll help me, I'll make sure that you get out of this whole con free and clear. You'll have your baby and you can do what you want."

"What're you talking about? How can you help me? You still with the Pinks?"

"Did they use you to trap Henry Cummings?"

She sighed. "No. They used a woman from town here. She's a beauty. Sort of crazy and violent sometimes. But she sure managed to get Cummings to give up everything and come out here with her."

"What's her name?"

"Serena Hopkins."

Another name on the list.

"The list is getting shorter."

She gave a small snort. "You still keep lists."

"They work."

"I can still picture you sitting up in your drawers at the table in the middle of the night. New Orleans was so hot. You'd be rolling cigarettes and writing up your reports and the sweat would be rolling off you. We had some good times."

"Yeah," I said, "sure sounds like it."

She laughed. "Well, maybe I chose the wrong example. But I do have fond memories of us."

Why ruin a sentimental moment with the truths of betrayal and deception?

She faced the road again. Lifted the reins. "I need to get into town, Dev."

And then she set off to town.

FOUR

I was walking back from the livery when a massive hand grabbed my shoulder. I didn't have the sense that this was supposed to cause me pain. It was simply supposed to slow me down.

I turned around. He looked a lot cleaner and smelled a lot better than he had the other night. He'd also lost the craziness in his eyes. He wore a well-cut brown suit with a snappy yellow cravat. I'll bet he made his police chief father damned proud of him.

"You remember me?" he said. He sounded awful merry about it. As if we were old friends.

"I dimly recall smashing a whiskey bottle across your face."

"And then you sapped me several times."

"If you want an apology, Earle, you're out of luck. You had it coming. You beat the hell out of that girl."

"You got me wrong there, Mallory." He was so big it was like standing in front of a massive tree and trying to have eye contact with the highest branch. "I want to apologize to *you*." His hand clasped mine. Overlapped it.

"Like I said, you beat up a girl. She's the one you should apologize to."

"Oh, hell. She knew I'd be around next day and give her triple what she normally gets. I guess she gets a little scared when I get to whalin', but I've never really done any damage to her."

There wasn't much use arguing with him. He was like Cora, I supposed. He wanted to banish all bad memories. I took out my watch from my vest pocket, tapped it. "I'd better be moving along, Earle."

I'm not sure I can adequately describe his next expression. It gave the impression of superiority, the way I always sensed that Cora was holding back something important. I saw that in his eyes now. And when he smirked, I knew I was right.

"He never mentioned me, did he?"

"Who are we talking about here, Earle?"

"Your friend Wally Tomkins."

My entire body tensed. I needed a few seconds to take in the implications of what he'd just said.

"I don't know any Wally Tomkins."

The smirk remained. "I didn't figure you did, Mallory. I didn't figure you did."

Then the smirk vanished. "You want to stand here and try and bullshit me or go into that café over there and have a serious discussion?"

The place was packed with laughing ladies in lavish picture hats, a garden of colorful ribbons atop them.

I had coffee. So did Earle.

"I figure you're what he was."

"And that would be what, Earle?"

"Some kind of *federale*. I'm not sure what kind yet. But I think you're the same, whatever it is."

"Wally didn't talk to you. He wouldn't."

"He didn't have to. I used to work for the telegraph company here. One of the many jobs the old man got me so I'd 'stay out of trouble' as he always puts it. But they fired me for coming in late all the time." He tapped his skull. "Liquor to blame, they said. Stupid bastards. I could get more work done in an hour than they could a whole shift. Anyway, the telegrams Wally got usually came from Washington, D.C. And over a couple of months, I was able to figure out that they were about some fella named Cummings and some plates for printing money."

He drank some of his coffee.

"Then he started getting telegrams from

'The Boss' saying he was sending a Dev Mallory out here. You."

More coffee. Then he sat back in his chair and lighted a cheroot. He exhaled a big bankerly puff and said, "Then I started following him around. Didn't take too long to figure out what was going on. The whole counterfeiting setup, I mean. At that point, I even found out where Cummings was."

I didn't want to look or sound excited. I just said, "But now Wally's dead and you don't know where Cummings is anymore and you're worried that you're not going to get any of that counterfeit to pass all over the West."

"You're right about Wally. He's dead. And you're right about my wanting to get my hands on that counterfeit. But you're wrong about Cummings. I know exactly where he is. I'm just waiting for the right time to go there and nab him. And his plates."

This was turning into an improbable day. Two people bringing me completely up to date on what had been going on here. I knew what Cora wanted — a new life, baby, and husband. I wondered what Earle wanted.

He said, "If you were just plain old law,

140

I'd go after the plates myself. But you *federales* . . . I don't want to be hounded the rest of my life." He made a thoughtful face and said, "Is there a reward for Cummings and the plates?"

"Ten thousand dollars."

He whistled. "Impressive." Then he smiled. "But you know what would be even *more* impressive?"

"Fifteen thousand dollars?"

"I was actually thinking more like twenty."

"I don't set the rewards, Earle. The government does."

"You could wire them. Tell them you've got a sure thing if they'll double the reward."

"I feel sorry for your old man, Earle."

A grin. "Having a son like me?"

"Yeah."

"Hell, even the old lady, when she was alive, she couldn't take him, either. Big man and his copper uniform. All his talk about his days in the Army."

"You're quite the boy, Earle. Your old man seems all right."

"Yeah, sure. A barrel of laughs."

"Think about something here, Earle. There may be something going on here neither one of us understands right yet."

"Yeah, like what?"

"Like Arthur Davis dying."

"He had an accident."

"Did he? You sure of that?"

I wanted to trouble him a little. Undermine his peacock confidence.

I stood up. "I'll see you around, Earle."

He grabbed my wrist with iron fingers. "You going to send that telegram? Get me twenty instead of ten?"

I ripped my hand from his hold. "I guess we'll just have to wait and see, won't we?"

FIVE

Serena Hopkins lived in a large but shuttered Spanish-style house. All those windows facing the sun — and on such a sunny day, too — but to no purpose. What had probably been a show house not long ago was starting to fall into niggling kinds of disrepair. The grass needed cutting, the hedges needed trimming, and the decorative iron fence that ran waist-high around the quarter-acre plot had a front gate that hung crooked. The walk was missing pieces of flagstone, and several of the gutters on the eaves had come loose.

She didn't answer until I damned near kicked the door in. But she was worth the wait. She had the kind of sulky erotic looks the French seem to prefer in their young women. She wasn't exactly young, wasn't exactly old, but that point was moot. She'd probably be a seductive corpse. She wore a tight pink shirt tucked into jeans. My crotch got tight out of sheer respect for a sensual lady. It wasn't difficult to understand why old Arthur Davis had liked hanging around her. The golden catlike eyes gave me a little trouble. She looked at me with a mixture of distrust and confusion. I'd once tracked a man into an asylum. A lot of the inmates had worn the same kind of eyes.

"You think I'm deaf?" she half-shouted at me. "Why'd you have to knock so loud? You scared all my kitties."

"Well, when you didn't answer the first sixty-two knocks, I thought I'd have to up the ante a little bit."

She obviously didn't find me humorous.

By now, the odors from inside the house were drifting out into the open air. She hadn't been kidding about cats. Plural. The house also reeked of grime and long-ago meals, the way tenements do. And the unmistakable odor of cat urine.

I eased my way inside. Given a choice between sleeping in the backyard and sleeping in here, I'd take the backyard. The house, once fine, was now a museum of various odors and frayed furniture and tiny land mines of kitten turds. The kittens were everywhere, everywhere. Couch, chairs, tabletops, magazine piles, even clinging to the heavy, dusty drapes. They were cute enough, but they would be a whole hell of a lot cuter if she'd taken the trouble to keep her house clean.

The other thing was the paintings. Terrible framed canvases of her at a young age in various ballerina outfits. The painter should have his hands cut off so he could never defile a canvas — and human sensibility — again.

"Did you hear about Arthur Davis?" I said.

"Who are you?"

"My name's Mallory."

Her expression was one of disgust. "Yes, I've heard what happened to him. We didn't end up all that well. He was the first man who ever cheated on me." She was Cleopatra, apparently. All men bent to her will. But with those eyes and lips and that still-sumptuous body, I could see her point. Davis would have had to look hard to find a worthy replacement for her.

I told her about my talk with Cora and that Cora recommended that I talk to her. "He was murdered. It wasn't an accident."

Disgust changed to fear. Her voice got shaky. "You think I don't know that? That makes three of us he's killed."

"He?"

"He, she, they, it. Somebody's killing us. That's all that matters."

"Cora seems to think that it's one of you

in the ring itself. That somebody decided to get it all for himself."

"Maybe."

She walked over to the fireplace mantel. A small portrait of her as a ballerina stood on the far right edge. A kitten lay on her side, dozing, next to it.

"Why do you say 'maybe'?"

She snapped, "Because I don't know what else to say. Because I've thought about these murders so long I get a headache the minute the subject comes up. I just got a headache now."

"Who else could it be?"

"Did you hear what I said? I said I have a headache. At this point, a gentleman would say that he was sorry I wasn't feeling well. And then he'd leave."

"He, she, it, they is going to kill again. Maybe much sooner this time. Maybe you this time."

We were interrupted by a white kitten that couldn't have been more than a few weeks old. She walked between the woman's legs and rubbed her head against an ankle. Serena reached down and picked her up. When she was upright, holding the kitten protectively against her shoulder, she said, "What's your interest in all this, anyway?"

146

Time for a useful lie. "The first man who was killed — Lakin — was my first cousin. His wife sent me here to see what I could find."

The kitten licked her neck a few times with a quick pink tongue. "They get hungry all the time. Their poor mother can't keep up with them. So I put out a little milk to help them along."

"That's nice."

She glanced around. "This place really needs a good cleaning, doesn't it?"

It was as if she went in and out of reality. She seemed to have forgotten about everything else — counterfeiting, dead men, and a stalking killer.

"Well, it could use a little dusting, I guess," I said.

"If I ever get any money again, I'll not only clean this place, I'll have a party. A big one. Invite everybody. Even Vince Kelly. You know Kelly?"

I laughed. "Better than I want to sometimes."

"He's been sniffing around here. He keeps trying to get me into bed. I have to say he's awfully cute. But I don't want to give him the upper hand. You give men the upper hand, they always end up slapping you with it." Then: "I was quite beautiful when I was younger. I also had style. *Au courant,* as they say. My papa sent me all the way to New York to study dance. I was quite good at it." The feral face tautened beneath the piled blond hair. "But I met a man. He was one of the dancers. Those men don't usually care for women in the way most men do. But he cared for me. At least I thought he did." The kitten started licking just under her jaw. She giggled, and in that moment she was sixteen or seventeen again and sane and perfect. "I'm ticklish there and she knows it. Isn't it funny? That a little white kitten would know my ticklish spot? I do believe she's got the devil in her. But where was I?"

"The man you met at dancing school."

"Oh, yes. Stephen. I let him get the upper hand. And he not only slapped me with it, he stole from me with it. Oh, I let him, of course. I'd get money from my papa — who was quite a generous man — and Stephen would take a good share of it and then disappear for days. He'd come back smelling of opium and sex. Women have one kind of sexual odor and men another. His odor was women, and I must say they didn't seem to be the kind who worried much about cleanliness. I had to start asking Papa for more and more money to satisfy Stephen. Papa got suspicious. He wired a confidential agent to start following me and seeing what I was up to. Stephen was practically living at my apartment, for one thing. He couldn't afford one of his own. It didn't take long for the confidential agent to figure out what was going on. Papa sent my uncle Karl to get me. Uncle Karl was a very stern and angry man. He broke Stephen's jaw, closed up my apartment, told the landlady to give away all my belongings, and then got me on a train. He said that if I tried to run away, he'd handcuff me to him. Uncle Karl never bluffed. So I came back here — that was fifteen years ago — and here I've been ever since. The counterfeiting scheme — I planned a sort of comeback with the money I'd make on that." Then: "Did you notice the paintings of me in my ballerina outfits?"

I wanted to say, yes, I'd noticed every single one of the twenty-six in this room alone. "Yes."

"Stephen did those. The sad thing is that he had to be such a cad. I think he really had artistic talent, don't you?"

"Yes," I said, "artistic talent. Yes, indeed."

"I suppose I should give those paintings to a museum someday."

A museum for the blind, maybe. I just hoped dear Stephen was better at being a cad than he was at being an artist.

"You went to Washington," I said, "and convinced Henry Cummings to leave his family and come out here. But now nobody can seem to find him — or the plates."

"Sometimes, I feel guilty about it," she said. "About having an affair with him so he'd come to Denver with me. It didn't take him very long to regret it. I think he tried to run away. But Lakin and his friend Nick Byrd — they made it clear to him that if he went back home, he'd spend the rest of his days in federal prison. He started printing the money for them, but I think he really felt trapped. He didn't care for me anymore, either. I sort of felt sorry for him — he's almost sixty, he doesn't know anybody, he knows he made a terrible mistake — so I'd slip out and see him sometimes. But he didn't want anything to do with me. I think I reminded him of all the mistakes he made."

She was a bright, perceptive woman. In addition to being a bluntly seductive one. "You were going to be one of the people who passed the money?"

She nodded. "Me, your cousin Lakin,

Byrd, and Arthur. Hit four states with big cities in a two-week period. Pass a million dollars of the stuff. And then divide up the spoils."

"What's Kelly's role in all this?"

She laughed. "According to him, since he came up with this idea of stealing Cummings and getting his hands on those plates, he was the mastermind. In other words, he thought his work was done. When the money was printed. He's not too happy now, though. No Cummings, no plates, and a million dollars in the best counterfeit ever made. And he can't find it anywhere. He seems to think Cummings might have run off with it all."

"Maybe," I said. "But here's something else to think about. Maybe Cummings decided to take everything and hide. But what if Cummings is the one who's killing you people? Have you ever thought of that?"

"God," she said, in a shocked voice. "God Almighty. Of course. Cummings hates us all." And then it came to her. "Especially me. I'm the one who tricked him into coming out here."

On the walk back to my hotel, I saw Nan Julian coming out of the grocery store. She was small enough to make the box she was carrying look huge.

"Stocking up for the winter?" I said. "I'll carry that as far as my hotel."

"Thanks, it's heavier than I thought."

"It's heavier than *I* thought."

"I decided to fix supper for everybody in the apartment house. It's gotten pretty lonely without Wally there."

I smiled. "You're quite the girl."

We'd reached my hotel.

"You could always drop by," she said. "There's plenty for everybody."

"You could feed a couple of platoons with this box."

"Do you like apple pie with cheese? That's how we'll finish the meal."

I leaned over and kissed her on the forehead. "I may just take you up on that. I'll sure try, anyway."

By coincidence, he was waiting for me in the lobby of my hotel. He made no secret of it. He had a book to keep him company, but he kept glancing up at the steady run of people in and out of the hotel doors.

When he saw me, he dog-eared his book and stood up. He always wore conservative suits to try and disguise his reckless nature. But nothing could disguise it. It was inherent in the swagger, in the amused dark eyes, in the easy sneer. You could dismiss him but even if you did, he'd leave you feeling lesser. He was just one of those people who'd always be two jumps ahead of you. A sizable number of people — enough to fill, say, Maine — had tried to kill him or have him killed. It was devoutly to be wished that somebody would succeed. And soon.

"I'll bet you never thought you'd see me again," he said, the gaudy smile brilliant in the handsome face. He was a bit overweight now, at least. It was some small comfort, anyway.

"I saw you yesterday," I said. "With Cora."

His instant reaction was anger. The hands at his sides coiled into fists and the dark eyes got cold as distant stars. But then the smile again. He even forced a couple of laughs. "Well, sorry to disappoint you, Dev. I mean, with her just a few days from hatching the little one, we couldn't put on a show for you. A little kissing, a little petting. She wouldn't even use her hand on me. She's taking this mother shit very seriously."

"She wants a kid."

"Yeah, well, she wanted a kid when I knocked her up, too. She lost that one." He tried to gauge the effects his words had on me. He made a helpless gesture with his hands. "Yeah, happened to me, too. I signed on for six months or so with her myself. She's a rough ride. She was like going out with myself — you never knew what she was really up to and she went to bed with anybody who caught her fancy. I'd never been in that position before — I was always the one in charge — and I sure didn't like it. Now, it doesn't mean anything to me. She's just somebody to work with. I saw her a little while ago. She said she told you all this. She said all you want is the plates and Cummings. You don't care about the rest of us. She thinks you must be federal now." He laughed. "The Pinks didn't do you any good. They set you on that path of righteousness and that means you're broke, if I'm not mistaken."

"I don't want to cut in. I just want the plates and Cummings. She's right."

"Now that's a pisser, isn't it? We had everything ready to go — and then it all vanished. And on top of it, somebody's killing us off. That's a sure-thing pisser where I come from."

"I'll make you the same offer I made Cora. You help me get the plates and

Cummings, I'll personally see to it that you won't be charged."

But he was the old Kelly. "I'll find him before you do, Mallory. I've worked too hard on this to just walk away from all that loot." And he gave me an old-Kelly salute, a jaunty routine he'd done all the years I'd known him. "Good luck to you, Mallory."

I grabbed the sleeve of his suit jacket. "Oh, I almost forgot. I just met a friend of yours."

"And who would that be?" He knew I was going to give him some grief.

"Serena Hopkins."

"Crazy bitch. You see those paintings of her as a ballerina?"

"Good old Kelly. You conquered yet?"

"I haven't gotten into her knickers yet. But it won't be long. Old Vince won't let you down." He winked. I happen to hate people who wink, especially people like Kelly who wink. "Maybe I'll start painting her."

"I didn't tell her this, Kelly. But you could be the killer. You take care of a few of them and then the others'll just pull out. And you'll have everything for yourself. And they won't know anything because you didn't run away with the plates and all that queer money. You waited them out."

"Say, this must be exciting for you," he said. "A *federale* and a detective at the same time." That fucking smile. "If there's any way I can help you, you be sure and let me know."

He walked away.

The evening came quickly. Before going to Natalie's room to fetch her for dinner, I went down to the taproom for a couple of quick beers. I'd now met everybody involved in the counterfeit plan. They were easy enough to assess. Except for Kimble and Cora, they'd gotten in for the chance of a lot of money. Now, with the killer in the mix, they'd be happy just to survive.

I was on my second beer when he came in. He looked more like a young Pink than a city cop, but a city cop he was, slim, scared Irisher with a derby and a cigar burning low in the corner of his mouth. The hat and the stogie were meant to make him look older and tougher. He put on a good show for the people who didn't know what they were seeing. He probably had a rep in town as a tough guy. Customers moved out of his way instinctively. He burrowed his way between me and another customer at the bar and angled himself so that I could see the badge he flashed

156

on the backside of his suit coat lapel. He did everything he could to look mean except strike matches on his teeth. But he didn't scare me because I saw the tic under his right eye start working when he got within four feet of me. I watched all this in the mirror behind the bar.

"You'd be Mallory," he said without taking the cigar stub from his mouth.

"I'd be Mallory." Still not turning around.

"A little somethin's come up and the chief wants to talk to you."

"I'm meeting a lady for supper. Tell the chief I'll talk to him later."

"Now. We go now, asshole. Right now. You understand?" If you didn't notice that the tic was getting even worse, you'd think he was probably just as fierce as he sounded.

I set my beer down and turned completely around and faced him. The drinkers around us moved away. They sensed a fight coming, as I did.

He reached in the left-hand pocket of his cheap suit coat and brought out something that gleamed in the lamplight. "You know what these are, smart boy?" He slid the brass knucks on over a taut, small hand. "You give me any more bullshit, I'm gonna bust that handsome face of yours."

"That's kind've funny, actually," I said.

He glared at me, tightened his grip on his knucks.

"Because," I said, slipping my hand into my own suit coat pocket and bringing out my own knucks, "I was thinking the same thing. And you know what? I'll bet I've got a lot more experience with my knucks than you've had with yours." This seemed like a good time for a little bullshit. "In fact, in Denver one time, some loudmouth deputy asshole pulled a knife on me and so I put on the knucks. And the doc who showed up with the police was pretty sure I killed him. Took him eleven hours to come out of it."

Now, I'm no expert on tics. Maybe someday if I get the time, I'll make a study of them. But his tic became a thing of ugly beauty. You could almost feel sorry for him if he was trying so hard to be tough. But I was sick of Chief Yancy and his ways and I was damned sick of this hayseed deputy.

"You boys gonna do anything in here," the bartender said, "I'm gonna run a tab on anything you break. You keep that in mind. And Dylan, I don't give a shit if you're wearin' a badge or not. You're gonna pay, too."

"Stay out of this," Dylan said. But his voice had a tremor in it and that tic was threatening to rip a patch of skin right off.

"This is gonna be one good sumbitch of a fight," I heard a gambler say. "Both of them wearin' them knucks like that." I hate people who take pleasure in the suffering of others.

And that was what changed my mind for me. They wanted a show. And screw them. They wanted a show, they could put one on for themselves.

I said, "Kid, I'm gonna go to see the police chief with you. But I'll tell you what. You make one more dumb-ass tough-guy remark to me, and I'm gonna take these knucks and pound your fucking face in to the point where not even your mother would recognize you. You got that?"

He gulped. He stammered. And his tic went into full speed.

I put my fist and my knucks in his face and said, "Now you lead the way and I'll follow. But you just remember what I said."

"Hey, he's backin' Dylan down," a fat man said.

I walked over to him and put my hand in his face same as I had with the kid. "You want some of this, lard ass?"

"No, sir."

"Then keep your fucking mouth shut. The kid's just learning. But I'll bet five gold eagles he can kick the hell out of any man in this room." I looked around at the faces. They were the kind of faces you saw at hangings and cockfights and shootouts, faces that grinned like evil children when death was at hand. "Anybody want to take that bet?" I scanned their faces again. "I figured not."

"C'mon," I said to the kid.

About three feet past the batwings, I said, "What the hell's the hurry about seeing the chief, anyway? I just talked to him yesterday."

"You talked to him about one thing yesterday. This is about another thing. A different thing."

"I get to know what this is about?"

He shrugged. "No harm in that, I guess. He thinks you murdered his son."

"What the hell're you talking about?"

"His son Earle. Somebody backshot him in an alley about forty-five minutes ago. I'll go along with you to tell your lady friend you won't be able to make supper tonight." He seized my bicep with strong fingers. "Let's go."

PART THREE
Lawrence Kenneth Kimble

One time at a regional banking convention in Cheyenne, Larry Kimble stepped out of the main hall to send a telegram back home. When he returned to the hall, he found that the speaker had finished and that everybody had broken up into small groups replete with liquor and cigars.

His group — he thought of it this way because they all came from Denver or closely surrounding towns — stood off to the side in the rear of the large hall. As he approached, he heard the men laughing. And the closer he got, the easier it was to figure out what they were laughing *about*. Him. When he stuttered. A man named Al Curtin was putting on the stuttering act and amusing the hell out of his fellow bankers.

When one of the men happened to notice Larry, the man stage-whispered to Al Curtin to shut up. Al, who had polished this act over many years, did not like to be interrupted by a squirt half his age and a quarter of *his* bank assets. But then Al glimpsed Larry there and said, "Hey, Larry, come on and have a drink with us."

The rest of the men just stood there looking guilty. At least a little bit of Larry Kimble died that afternoon. The nasty imitation took him back to his schoolyard days. He had always hated being asked a question by his teacher because he invariably stuttered when he spoke. He got so self-conscious that he brought the stuttering on himself. And then at recess and lunch he'd hear the boys imitating him, taunting him. He was shocked when he found that a few of the girls imitated him, too. He had always considered women smarter and more compassionate than men. On balance, they were. But still, there were some of them — It was a discovery he wished he'd never made.

In his hotel room that night, alone, half-drunk, he cried. Al Curtin's cruel imitation had unmanned him. He was a boy again, and boy-vulnerable to every slight and taunt. They had made fun of him all his life and they always would. When people would say to him, "You have everything, Larry," he'd always nod in agreement. He sure seemed to have everything. The bank he'd inherited from his father, respect of the important people of Denver (though they let him know in various subtle ways that they did not consider him a peer, as the Brits liked to call social equals), and an enviably beautiful if somewhat mysterious wife in Cora.

But none of that mattered when people mocked him. He wanted to skulk away and hide in some dark and dusty forgotten corner of the universe where he would never have to hear their imitations of him again. By himself. Because he knew that being the object of scorn made him lesser even in the eyes of those who cared for him. He didn't want pity; pity was too often what people offered in lieu of respect.

The incident at the banking convention affected him for a long month after. He couldn't sleep, he lost weight, and worst of all, he couldn't sustain an erection with Cora. She would always gently ask what was troubling him — she was careful to say that not being able to make love was not important; and he suspected that she was being sincere — but how did you tell the woman you loved so much, the woman you'd built your entire life around, the woman who'd brought you so much joy and self-esteem . . . How did you tell her that you became a weak little child when people made fun of you?

He was to feel this same kind of torment a few years after when a man who introduced himself as Ted Nealon visited his office one blustery November afternoon.

"There's just something about him I don't care for," whispered his secretary when she came into Kimble's office to announce the Nealon man.

Kimble smiled. "You say that about an awful lot of people."

"True. And if you think about it, I'm usually right."

He couldn't see what she was talking about. True, Nealon was a bit too smooth of tongue, a bit too insistent of charm, and a bit too pretty of face. But whatever it was the secretary had sensed — Larry Kimble just didn't see.

Until, of course, this Nealon, after talking about looking for a bank as he was new to Denver, said, smiling of course, "Are you ready for me to cut the bullshit, Kimble?"

"I beg your pardon."

"The bullshit, Larry. You'll forgive me for calling you Larry, but I guess I picked that up from Cora."

"My wife? What's she got to do with this?"

"Just stay calm, Larry." The friendly open smile had become a sneer. "Don't you worry about us sleeping together. Those days are long behind us."

"W-what's th-this ab-bout?" Kimble demanded. Or tried to demand. It was difficult to be forceful when you were stuttering.

"She never mentioned that you stuttered."

Idiotic as it was, the man's words made Kimble sentimental about his wife. She hadn't betrayed him. Not about the stuttering, anyway.

"She doesn't want to be any part of this," the slick man across the desk said. "She begged me to say that to you. She actually seems to be in love with you." The sneer. "And you stutter. Now that's a surprise, her ending up with somebody like you, Larry. But you know what? I'm sure glad she did. Because without you, my plan wouldn't work. I need somebody connected real good in the banking business. And that would be you, Larry. That would be you."

"I s-still d-don't know why you th-think I'll h-help y-you."

"Oh, Larry. You mean she didn't tell you?"

165

Kimble said nothing. Sat back in his leather executive chair, feeling vulnerable and helpless as a child. Wanting to blurt out terrible things to this arrogant sonofabitch. But not blurt them out in stuttered words.

"That little wife of yours, Larry. She's had some past. Now don't worry. I'm not going to sit here and tell you everything she's gotten those long, lovely hands of hers into. I'll just give you one example. We — the two of us, Cora and I — were working a robbery one time and everything was going just fine until Cora got real nervous — which wasn't like her, not at all — anyway, she gets real nervous, see, and she thinks this guard is going to do something — maybe go for his gun or something — and so she fires her own gun off in his direction. Now, Larry, there's something you have to understand. She's not a violent gal. I had never seen her even fire a gun until that very moment. So when she told me later that she didn't have any thought of killing the poor bastard — well, I believed her. I really did.

"Nearly every robbery — and I've been in on more than a few of them — some little thing will happen that'll spook the hell out of you. Make you panic the way it did Cora. And if it's just the wrong moment, and you're in just the wrong mood, you get spooked the way Cora did and you shoot. You don't mean to kill. You just shoot. Just try to scare the other guy is what it comes down to, Larry. But sometimes the bullet doesn't go where you expect it to. It's just like it's got a mind of its own. The damned bullet just flies out of the barrel and lights where it wants to light. In this guard I'm talking about, it lands right in his chest. Right next to his heart. And he dies before we can even get out of there.

"I kept my wits about me and made sure we got the money. But Cora — she just kind've went crazy. Kind've running around in circles, throwing the gun away like it was a poisonous snake or something, kneeling over the guard and screaming for him to wake up. Now I had one hell of a time getting her out of there, believe me. One *hell* of a time. So I guess in that way you owe me. If I hadn't kept my wits about me, you wouldn't have your own little Cora to love, honor, and obey, now, would you?"

"I'm n-not s-sure I b-believe you."

"Sure you're sure you believe me, Larry. You just don't *want* to believe. But take your time. Go home and ask little Cora about me. I'm using Ted Nealon while I'm out here. Don't want anybody to learn about my sordid past, Larry. Almost as sordid as little Cora's."

"W-What d-do you w-want f-from me?"

"You're looking at it in the wrong way, Larry. You've got to be more positive. I saw those fliers of yours out there about self-reliance and thinking positive about things. And here's an example of that for you. Your own philosophy, Larry. Your own philosophy. In fact, if I get the time, I think I'll come and hear you speak. I'm sure that would be worthwhile, Larry, a man like you. Worthwhile through and through.

"Now here's what's going on, Larry. I have gotten my hands on the actual plates they use in Washington, D.C., to produce one-hundred-dollar bills. And you know what else I've gotten my hands on, Larry? The man who engraved those plates himself. And he knows a lot about paper stock, ink, and printing. He started out in a print shop, in fact, when he was younger. I'm a dumb shit, Larry, and I'm the first to admit it. What I do is bring smart people together. The one kind of smart person I still need in this friendly little group of ours is a banker. Having our own bank'll come in handy when we start distributing one million dollars in queer money everywhere west of the Mississippi — and do it fast before anybody official knows what the hell is going on. You're going to be an even richer man than you are today, Larry. One hell of a lot richer."

ONE

"You were in that café forty minutes and all you talked about was baseball?" Chief Yancy said.

I don't suppose anybody ever wrote down a set of rules for mourning your dead child. People can really surprise you, the way they react to things. But Yancy's sole emotion was anger and suspicion. He seemed convinced that I'd killed his son. Given my fight with Earle in the whorehouse, it was probably reasonable to include me on a list of suspects. But it should have been a long list. Earle wasn't exactly a beloved figure in Denver.

And wedged in between the rage and accusations, I would've expected at least a moment or two of sorrow, of grief, of paternal woe. But we might have been talking about the death of a vagrant. He was that cold.

We were in Yancy's office. The door was closed. I'd been here long enough to smoke three cigarettes.

He sat his ass on the edge of his desk

and said, "He wanted in on it, didn't he?"

"In on what?"

"Whatever you're in on, Mallory. Whatever brought you out here."

"I told you. We talked about baseball."

He made a face. "You wondering why I'm not all broken up over my one and only child having just been murdered?"

"I guess that crossed my mind."

"That's because I knew what he was. And it wasn't nice, what it was. And it didn't come from his mother and it didn't come from me. You know something — and this is no bullshit, Mallory — you've heard of how they've switched babies in hospitals? I wondered about that all his life. He was getting in trouble when he was seven. His mother wouldn't let him play in the yard one day because he had a bad cold. So he smashed her kitten's head in with a rock and then set the kitten on fire."

"Boys will be boys."

"You think that's funny?"

"I just don't think it has anything to do with me."

"C'mon, Mallory, you know as well as I do that a seven-year-old who thinks like that — well, there's something wrong with him."

"As I said, I don't see what any of this has to do with me."

"You don't, huh?"

He stood up and walked over to a new wooden filing cabinet. From the bottom drawer he extracted a file. He brought it back and dropped it on the desk. It made a noise like a gunshot. It was a heavy file.

"This is Earle's police file. I was able to keep him from going to prison because the mayor likes me and so does the district attorney. They almost always found ways we could spare Earle time in prison. But it was getting harder. He was a criminal around the edges, as they say. Nothing bad enough that I couldn't control. Until recently. There was a bank robbery up on the Idaho border about six months ago. He was too cheap to pay rent anywhere else so he lived at home with me. Under his bed one day I found one of the bank bags from that robbery. You want to see a father start crying? You want to see a father be overwhelmed with grief and remorse? I didn't do any of that tonight because there wasn't any left in me. When I found that bank bag, I just sank down on his bed and cried like a baby. I just thanked God his mother wasn't here to see what he was turning into. He hated his mother — the sweetest woman you can imagine. And you can ask anybody about her. Rich, poor, white, colored, red — everybody liked her because she was sweet. Because she was good. She helped people all the time. And he hated her. Used to steal the little money she was able to save up. He spit in her face once because she wouldn't let him go out one night when he was thirteen. And the filthy names he called her — And she wouldn't let me beat him. That's all I ever wanted to do since he was seven or eight. Beat him. But she wouldn't let me. All I could do was slap him across the bottom a couple of times. There was no controlling him after he turned twelve or so." He tapped the file. "And one more thing. You know what?"

"I get the feeling you're going to surprise me."

"You're damned right I'm going to surprise you. He hated baseball. Always had. Thought it was tedious. Football was his game. But I doubt he ever sat through an entire baseball game in his life. And you're telling me you sat there and talked baseball."

He went back around his desk. Sat down. Opened the left top drawer. Took out his pipe. Started playing with it.

"So what lie are you going to tell me this

time, Mallory? You've had a minute to think it over. Baseball won't wash, but by now you've probably come up with a better one."

"I was wrong. I guess it was football we talked about."

"Uh-huh."

"Or maybe astronomy. He said he was interested in astronomy."

He disregarded me.

"He was very intense, lately. He was focusing on something. I'd never seen him like that before when he visited. Usually, he didn't let anything occupy his time other than having fun. And making a little money — usually dishonest money — so he could afford that fun. But this was different. He'd sit in a chair in our front room and just stare out the window. And sometimes, he'd take my field glasses from my bedroom drawer. They were the ones I used in the war. Maybe you can tell me what he was up to."

"Afraid I wouldn't know."

Yancy scowled. "He was smart, you know. His mother and I both graduated high school and so did he. And we always had plenty of books and magazines around for him to read. He was smart enough to wait for the big thing that was going to make him rich. And I can't shake the feeling that that involved you somehow."

"If it involved Earle and me working together, why would I kill him?"

He laughed bitterly. "Because you started hating him the way everybody else did. Because you found out he was going to cheat you somewhere down the line. Because he got in one of his moods and you couldn't take it and shot him."

"Awful generous of him to turn his back on me. Most people aren't that obliging when they think you're going to kill them." I put my hands on the arms of the wooden chair and stood up. "If you had anything that mattered, you'd have arrested me by now. You had your man drag me in here to see if you could learn something from me. But you can't because I don't know anything. We didn't talk about football or baseball, but we didn't talk about any big deal, either. We just talked, the way people do when they're killing time. He said he wanted to apologize to me for the other night in the whorehouse."

"Earle never made a sincere apology in his life."

"Well, then he didn't have anything better to do than sit around and drink coffee. That's all I know and likely all I'll ever find out. I don't know why he was killed or who killed him. All I know is that it wasn't me."

The eyes narrowed. "Don't make the mistake of thinking you're free and clear, Mallory. You're not. You're still my first choice for what happened to Earle."

"So long, Chief."

Natalie didn't answer my knock. I was almost ninety minutes late. I went into my room, lay on the bed rolling a couple of cigarettes and smoking them.

Earle's murder spooked me. He wasn't part of the counterfeit ring. But he did know — or so he claimed — where Henry Cummings was being held. For all his talk about what a terrible man Earle had been, Chief Yancy was going to find his killer. I'd had the sense back in his office that he really didn't consider me much of a suspect. But he did think I knew enough to put him on the path leading to the truth.

I'd considered telling him who I was and why I was in his city, but then I realized we'd be fighting each other as much as helping each other. His interest was his son; my interest was Cummings and the plates. If I had to let Earle's killer go free to get the plates and Cummings, I would.

And then there'd be hell to pay with Yancy.

I slept. I had a couple of bad dreams, but I couldn't remember anything about them when the knock came. I woke up disoriented for a moment. What room? What city? What assignment? You get that way after a while.

Then a second knock and I was winging my legs off the bed and rubbing my face. My mind bloomed with memories. Denver. A hotel room. Counterfeiting. Earle.

"Who is it?" I called out, reaching for my Colt holstered on the bedpost.

"Natalie."

"Are you going to shoot me?"

Her laugh was bright even through the door. "I probably should."

"Hold on a second."

I combed my hair with my fingers, pulled on trousers and shirt, took a pull of whiskey for my breath, and went to the door.

"I'm sure you have a good excuse, Dev."

"Believe it or not, I do. I was almost arrested."

She sat on a chair, pretty and proper in a dark brown dress that flattered her hair. She seemed amused. "Now that's original, at least. You must've worked on that a while."

177

"Unfortunately, it's true."

I told her about Earle Yancy's murder and my run-in with him the other night. I didn't mention that the run-in took place in a whorehouse.

"You're not having a very good time here in Denver."

"Not so far," I said. I sat on the edge of the bed, rolling a cigarette. "How about you? What'd you end up doing?"

"There was a musicale in the library. Not much of a crowd. But the music was very good. Relaxing." She made a face. "Getting me away from all this legal business, anyway."

"Your brother still not cooperating?"

"My attorney seems to think my brother may be off on another bender. His own lawyer doesn't seem to know where he is. And this is exactly why I want to keep brother dear from getting at his own money. He'll go through it in less than a year — and it's a good deal of money, believe me." The light tone faded now. Her face drew tight with anguish. "I love him. I want to protect him. That's my only interest in this. I have my own inheritance. I don't need his. But his lawyer wants to make me out as some kind of villain in this, as if I'm scheming to take my brother's money for myself. It gets tiring."

Just then, in the soft lamplight, she looked years older than she had before. Around the mouth especially. Tight, angry.

"Sometimes," she said, "I think maybe I should just let him get his inheritance and do what he wants to with it. If he wants to spend it on liquor and women and end up in the poorhouse, so be it."

"But you won't."

A broken smile. "Are you sure of that?"

"You believe in principle and goodness and duty."

This smile was full, the way it usually was. "My, you paint a noble picture of me."

"Not noble. Just dutiful. You believe in right and wrong and responsibility. He's your brother and you love him. And you feel responsible for him — no matter how painful that gets sometimes."

She sighed. "I guess that's right." She stared out the window. "Not me being noble and all. I'm not noble in the least. Part of it is family pride. And there's nothing noble about pride. I just don't want people to see us as drunken louts who can't hang onto their money."

I walked over to her and took her hand.

179

"But mostly it's because you love your brother and want to help him."

"Gosh." She laughed. "Maybe I really *am* noble, after all."

It happened, then. She was standing up and sliding into my arms. Our mouths opened quickly after what started out as a very chaste kiss. We kissed for a long time. Our bodies were fitting together nicely when she eased me away with fingertips on my chest.

"Whew," she said. "I really didn't expect anything like this."

"Neither did I," I said. "But I'm happy it happened."

She took my hand and led me to the bed. I was certainly ready. But we had different things in mind.

"May I — I'd just like to talk for a while, Dev. Sort of explain myself to you."

"Fine," I said. Of course a certain part of my body was acting up. It wasn't polite. It didn't care whether she wanted to talk for a while or not. It had its own ideas.

She took my hand and held it gently in her lap. She smelled awfully good. She looked awfully good. She was all female, every pore of her, and I was losing myself in her. I hadn't felt this kind of pure hard lust in a long, long time. My lust always

180

doubles or triples when there's real affection in the mix. . . . And I did like her.

Her forehead creased slightly and she said, "I'm going to be very honest with you, Dev. I've never been married. But I'm not a virgin. I was engaged for a long time and we slept together every chance we got. But then he got interested in another woman. I wasn't exactly left at the altar, but it wasn't easy for me. I really loved him, for one thing. And for another, I wasn't used to being a figure of pity. You know how people are. Good people, I mean, with the best of intentions. They mean to make you feel better, but they treat you as if someone in your family died. And they always say the same things. 'You'll meet someone else.' 'He wasn't any good, anyway.' 'You're a young woman. There's plenty of time to find a husband.' I always laughed about that one. Where I come from, if you're not married by eighteen, you're a spinster."

She put her head on her shoulder. "I'm not making fun of them, Dev."

"I know you're not."

"I say the same corny things to people. My sister broke off with her fiancé, and I must have told her so many times that she had plenty of time to meet a husband that she started charging me money every time I said it." A soft laugh. "She got rich."

The persistent little man down there still wasn't ready to concede the moment. His advice was to let her talk it all out and then lean her back and try and seduce her.

"He's the only man I ever slept with, Dev."

She was saying no. She was saying it in a way that made it impossible for me to push past this point. That wasn't her intention — she was honestly sharing her feelings — but that was the effect.

"I hope you understand, Dev."

I leaned over and kissed her.

"Think we could have dinner tomorrow night?" she asked.

"That's what I was thinking," I said. "And this time, I promise to show up."

She gave me a quick sweet kiss on the corner of my mouth. "You'd better," she said. And then smiled and left.

TWO

In the morning news sheet, I found Earle Yancy's address. Two trolley car rides got me there. The eight a.m. sunlight did the neighborhood no favors. The houses were the crudest clapboard, the workmanship just as crude. They were fairly new, too. The paint was the only thing that had held up much to the weather, and even so, you could see where large patches of it were already fading badly. You could even see raw wood in a few places. Several of the roofs already needed repairing. This was an area for transients who planned to stay for a month or two. I didn't see any kids or dogs or cats. What I did see were drummers toting heavy suitcases no doubt crammed with their wares. They set them down when they reached the corner where the trolley stopped. There were maybe a dozen of them and they seemed almost jolly. I wondered why. If there was a hell and I was sent to it, I know old Satan would make me spend eternity trying to sell things door to door. I couldn't sell anybody anything even if I held a gun on them.

The house I wanted was in the middle of the block. A chunky woman in a man's flannel shirt and baggy jeans was picking up broken glass, remnants of a whiskey bottle, from the front stoop. She didn't look happy about it. She muttered beneath her breath and shook her head several times before realizing that I was standing just a few feet away.

"Yeah?" she said. "I sure hope you ain't tryin' to sell me anything because I ain't in the mood. First I have to clean up where Mr. Duncan pukes all over when he comes in after his carousin' last night, and then this mornin' I find all this broken glass." She spit a brown stream of tobacco off the side of the front stoop. "There are some men that just shouldn't be allowed to drink, if you ask me."

"I guess I'd have to agree with that."

"So you ain't sellin' nothin'?" she said, checking to see if I was toting any wares.

"Ain't sellin' a thing," I said. "Just asking a few questions."

The eyes narrowed. The wide Slavic face took on a sudden meanness. "You ain'ta Pink, are you?"

"No, ma'am."

"Was a Pink helped send my husband to

prison. His third time. I'll never see him again. And every single time, they framed him. Every single time. Ouch! Sonofabitch!" She'd pricked herself on an edge of a glass shard. Nothing serious.

I was still trying to figure out the odds of somebody who'd been framed three times. Lots of men got framed. Coppers were often just as dirty as criminals, come to that. Once was believable. Twice was possible. But framed three times? Now you were dealing with great unlikelihood. To be kind.

I decided to make things simple for both of us. I had a nice new greenback in my right pocket. I took it out and handed it to her.

"I ain't got no vacancy."

"It's information I'm after."

"You a copper?"

"No."

"Well, if you ain't a copper and you ain't a Pink, why you askin' questions?"

"You want the money or not?"

She stared down at the money. "Hell, yes, I want it."

"Then tell me about Earle Yancy."

She laughed. "Hell, I shoulda seen that one comin'. Naturally, people'd be around, him gettin' murdered and all."

"Why would people be coming around for him?"

She squinted at me. "He was onto something."

"Onto what?"

"I'm not sure. But one day he come back here late at night and somebody was waitin' for him right by the door here. Two somebodies. They beat him up pretty bad. One of 'em had a gun on him and the other did the hittin'. Fair fight, Earle woulda ripped their heads off. Ain't many people coulda whipped Earle. Anyway, it woke me up and I come down with a shotgun and chased 'em off."

"You hear anything they said to Earle?"

"The one with the gun, he kept sayin', 'Where's Cummings?' over and over. And then when I come down, Earle said to the one with the gun, 'Gonna cost you ten thousand.' That's about all I was able to pick up on. I liked Earle. I took him inside and cleaned him up and fixed up his cuts well as I could, and then took him up to his room and put him to bed. That one man musta hit him for a long time. I even cleaned up his clothes for him. Best as I could, anyway. But they was so bad off, he ended up just throwin' that suit away."

"What was wrong with his suit?"

186

"Limestone. I could tell because the mister used to work at a quarry. It's got a special look if you know what you're seein'. Earle looked like he'd rolled around in it."

"Those men ever come back?"

"Not that I know of."

"Can you describe them?"

She shot another brown stream at the ground. The grass was sparse here, as if it had been seeded not too long ago. A good rain would turn the front yard into a mud puddle. I raised my head for a look at the snow-topped mountains in the distance. A person could sure learn to like Denver.

"One of 'em I can describe. The tall one. It was so dark, I couldn't really see the one with the gun at all."

Her description was so accurate, I recognized Kelly even before she'd finished up detailing what he'd looked like and what he'd worn.

"How about letting me see Earle's room," I said when she'd finished her description.

"Can't do it, mister. Chief Yancy was here late last night. He said nobody was to be let in there under no circumstances. He spent half an hour in there by hisself. Felt sorry for him."

I thought of how he'd pretended not to

care about Earle anymore. Blood's a bond you don't break easily. Even if you hate the bastard.

"Did he have any particular friends?"

"Earle?" She shrugged. "I suppose so. None he ever talked about especially, though. He did his drinking downtown. A lot of time he'd be drunk enough, he'd just flop in a cheap hotel. Oh — well, he did have a lady caller last week."

"Anybody you knew?"

"Didn't 'know' her. Seen her pitcher in the paper, though, a couple times."

"Why was she in the paper?"

"She runs that shelter for the street kids right down near the Catholic church. She's always asking folks for money. Don't think she gets much. The rich folks here are pretty tight when it comes to things like that." She grinned with several missing teeth. "Guess that's why they *have* so much money."

"Did she go up to his room?"

She gave me a stern eye. "Hell, no, she didn't. I let these men have gals up in their rooms, it'll turn into a whorehouse overnight."

"Did he come down to see her?"

"He wasn't home. I told her he might not be back till late or even the next day.

But she looked so damned mad, she said she'd sit right here on the stoop and wait for him. And that's exactly what she did."

"She say why she was mad?"

"Not to me, she didn't."

"He ever show up?"

"Yeah. Way after I went to sleep. She really tore into him. She's got some tongue on her, that one. Not dirty but angry. She ripped into him good."

"But you don't know why?"

"I kinda hinted around the next day about bein' curious and all, but he wouldn't say nothin' about it. He looked irritated I even brought it up. Called her 'bitch' underneath his breath. He had a pretty bad hangover."

She glanced at the pieces of broken bottle she held on a dustpan. "No offense, mister, I appreciate you payin' for my time and all, but I got a lot of work to do here. I do my washin' this time of the week."

"Well, this has been helpful. I appreciate it."

"He could be pretty mean, Earle could. But he was always pretty sweet to me. Even gave me a birthday box of candy this year. Right after them coppers framed my husband again. Tryin' to make me feel better, I guess, Earle was."

"Yeah," I said, trying to keep any trace of sarcasm from my voice, "that sounds like Earle, all right."

THREE

I found the building housing most of the city offices, and spent the next two hours there asking about areas in and around the city where there were large deposits of limestone. I ended up with a list of three possibilities. There were several more, but these were the major ones. I wrote down directions for all of them, and then went back to the livery stable for another horse.

The sun clouded over a little after one o'clock, and by one-thirty a fine, steady rain was trying its best to soak the poncho I'd bought just before visiting the livery.

I was maybe halfway to my first destination when I realized that the rider I kept glimpsing behind me every once in a while wasn't dropping away. On a main traveled road this wouldn't have been suspicious, but I'd taken so many shortcuts per the directions I'd been given that I realized he wasn't out for just a ride. He was following me.

When I reached the deep valley I was looking for, the rider sat his horse on a hilltop a good distance back of me. I watched him bring field glasses to his eyes. I pretended not to see him.

For a time I just sat my own horse and looked around. You don't find many places more beautiful than Colorado. The serene, shadowed foothills were covered with ash and aspen and fir trees; the ground was a carpet of brilliant green grama grass with daisies and wild irises and dogtooth violets strewn in random patterns across it. The breezes from the mountain were scented with the rippling water of clean mountain streams and the pines that stretched far up toward the peaks.

I resented the bastard following me. If he hadn't been here, I would have been able to enjoy the treasures of the place. I couldn't get a look at him. He'd moved behind some pines. All I could see was the head of his horse.

I decided to chase him away, at least temporarily. It was an old game the Marines taught us. Surprise is the word for it.

I lifted my Colt from its holster, turned my horse around, and started charging up the hill where the follower sat with his field glasses.

I wished I was closer to see his face.

192

He'd be wondering what the hell was going on. Here he'd been having it all his way, laying back and doing his spying at will, when all of a sudden this crazy sonofabitch comes charging up the hill and ruining all his fun.

He seemed paralyzed for a minute there, but then suddenly jammed his field glasses into his saddlebag, ripped his rifle from his scabbard, and started firing at me. He'd turned the surprise around on me. I was too far away to do any damage with my pistol. I jerked the reins of the horse to the right, and hung as far down on the shy side of the animal as I could as he ran toward grass long enough to hide me.

I reined him to a stop and then pitched myself to the ground. The landing hurt. I wasn't much of an acrobat and I was a long ways from being young enough to absorb that kind of punishment. I needed a full minute or two to deal with the pain. Then I slapped the horse away and started belly-crawling through the grass.

The horseman was no longer firing. He sat maybe a hundred yards away, field glasses scanning the long grass. He couldn't see me but I could see him. He wore a red bandanna over his face now.

If he saw me, he could kill me easily. I

was sure he'd reloaded. I was also sure that soon enough he'd see me and open fire. His horse kept drifting toward me, but the horseman was still out of range. Ten, fifteen feet closer was all I needed —

Then he spotted me.

The glasses got stuffed back in the saddlebag, the repeater reappeared, and the long metal barrel gleamed in the sunlight as its tip exploded in my direction.

I rolled and kept rolling, pausing only to see where he was in relation to me. I wouldn't have much of an opportunity to surprise him — two, three shots at most — so I had to be ready when the right moment came.

He did me an improbable favor. He charged me. Or at least he tried to charge me. He was off by maybe three or four yards. By the time he'd adjusted for his mistake, I was up in a crouch and firing at him. The advantage was still his. He wasn't close enough for me to be accurate even now and when my bullets started coming at him, he jerked his horse away and started back toward the hills.

By the time I got to my own horse and started after him, he wasn't much more than a silhouette against the sky. I rode hard enough to cut the distance considerably.

I had no intention of following him very far, but I made it seem as if I would. I emptied my Colt as I galloped behind him. He didn't return fire. He just headed for a deep stand of firs that he disappeared behind as soon as possible.

I loped back to the site where a tall hill looming over a narrow gorge offered a selection of limestone caves. A pronghorn antelope stood in a grassy glen watching me approach.

As it turned out, she didn't have much to see. The quarry was small, shallow, and narrow. Nobody was around and there were no tools in the bed of the quarry. The blasters hadn't had to go far down. The limestone, most of which was gray, was just below the surface.

I spent an hour there, but didn't find a damned thing.

The rest of the afternoon went the same way. Two more quarries, both of them of significant size, both of them swarming with busy workers. I talked to a couple crew bosses. One of them knew who Earle Yancy was, but had never seen him at the site. The other crew boss didn't know Earle, and made it clear that he didn't have time to talk. A Denver architect had changed his mind on some vast and imminent project. He now wanted limestone instead of what he'd had in mind before. And this crew boss damned well meant to give it to him. And on time.

By this time, my own clothes were almost as dusty as those of the workers. The horse was pretty dusty, too.

On the way back to the city, I kept watch for the follower. There hadn't been any sign of him since I'd chased him off. I had time to try and puzzle through where and how Earle had picked up so much limestone dust. I was assuming that the limestone dust connected in some way to Henry Cummings — if Earle had been telling me the truth about knowing where Cummings was. But maybe he'd been lying. And even if he was telling the truth, the limestone may not have had anything to do with Cummings, anyway.

At the moment, it looked as if I'd wasted most of the day.

FOUR

The St. Christopher Center was a wooden house of two stories that made up in cleanliness what it lacked in the grace of its design. No renowned architect had put this one together. The best they'd been able to afford apparently was an enthusiastic amateur. The screen door I knocked on, for instance, did not quite fit its frame. It didn't close flush in a couple of places. The steps I stood on canted to the right. And the putty used on the front window was too thick in some spots and too thin in others.

The woman who came to the door made up for any misgivings I had about the carpentry. Even through the screen door I could see her simple pale good looks — clean, open, almost winsome, but in a completely unaffected way. She wore a tan work shirt, jeans, and cowboy boots. She said, "Are you Mr. Severeid?"

"Afraid not. I'm Mr. Mallory."

"Is it him?" a girl called.

"Not yet, Doris. I'm sure he'll be along very soon." In a quieter voice, she said,

"She's a homeless girl. One of our benefactors invited her to his home tonight for a family dinner. She's really excited. Some of the rich people in this town are really generous."

"I heard the opposite."

"Well, some are, some aren't. I expect it's that way with every city."

"I expect it is." I smiled. "You afraid to come out from behind the door."

"Oh," she said. "That's very rude. Of course I'll come out. In fact, I'd like to walk around back and check our garden. I've been so busy today, I haven't had time."

She put forth a strong slim hand. "Gwen O'Hara."

I gave her my name. I didn't add anything else.

The sounds were what you'd imagine. On our way walking around the house — it was massive if nothing else — she told me that they had room to sleep twenty-five here, that the boys and girls had mostly been abandoned by their parents or were runaways from terrible situations, and that St. Christopher's parish, which was a block away, bought this corner property and had the men of the church build it over the course of three weekends. I didn't say that it looked like it, which I thought was damned nice of me.

Thus, the sounds from inside. Laughter, a guitar, a large dog barking, somebody shouting that somebody had taken his school pen, and two girls sitting in a screened window talking.

"Could be a hard place to concentrate in," I said.

"The noise? Oh, this is nothing. Only half the kids are here. Wait till supper time." She said this with an inspiring enthusiasm.

"How'd you come to be here?"

She just looked at me with that pale kid-face of hers and said, "My dad killed my mom when I was twelve. Then killed himself. We all saw it. I had to raise my little brother and sister. We mostly just had to make do on the street. There wasn't any place like this. I started going to Mass at St. Christopher's, and I met this old monsignor and started telling him what it was like on the street for kids. So he got the idea for this place. And he just planned all along that I'd run it for the church. I consider it a privilege."

"Your brother and sister here?"

"Oh, no." She grinned. "But that's a compliment in a way."

"It is?"

"Sure. Either you need glasses or you don't know how to judge a woman's age. My brother and sister are both in their twenties now. I'm almost thirty."

"You're joking."

"You may be a dangerous man, Mr. Mallory."

"How's that?"

"A woman could get used to your flattery."

The garden covered half of an enormous backyard. The half that wasn't given over to carrots, peas, corn, and other vegetables was clotted with a swing set, a couple of one-wheeled bicycles, and a chest overflowing with baseball mitts and bats and balls. A Mexican girl sat under a shade tree tending to her loom. A colored boy sat under a different shade tree reading a book while a fat little golden puppy sitting in his lap kept trying to lick his face. The racket from the house wasn't so loud back here. There was a serenity here, in fact. The colored boy could have been me when I was his age. My favorite stories were pirate ones back then.

Gardens are mysterious to me. I once helped my older sister plant some things one spring. Nothing I planted grew. She couldn't explain it. She watched me do my

200

planting and said I was doing everything correctly. But nothing grew. If I thought more deeply about things, my barren section of garden might have made me nervous about my soul. Maybe the earth knew something about me I didn't.

Gwen, on the other hand, haunched down several times between rows and did an awful lot of plucking, pruning, pushing, nudging, and watering from the spouted yellow can she'd brought along.

"You make it look easy."

"That's the only thing that keeps us alive sometimes," she said. "I planted a garden down by a railroad siding. I made it big enough so that the hobos could take things from it but there'd still be enough left over for us. It was good training for running St. Christopher's."

She set the water can next to the back steps and then said, "Would you like to sit down?"

"Thanks."

We sat on the bottom step. I'd dusted myself off as much as possible, but it hadn't improved my look much. Limestone dust doesn't go well with human skin.

"You look sort of official," she said.

I'd started rolling a cigarette. "Official?"

"Umm-hmm. You've just got that air

about you, even with all that limestone dust. I can't explain it any better than that. I guess that's why you scared me when I saw you in the door."

"I must really be ugly."

"Oh, you know better than that. It's just that — that official sense I got from seeing you in the door. People were always coming to our door when my dad was alive. People trying to collect money. He was just a workman, but he gambled. There was always somebody after him. He also got in trouble with the law a lot. This was before the police here had uniforms. Some of them wore suits. They just had a certain air about them — official — like yours. So, tell me, Mr. Mallory, am I wrong about you?"

I was saved by a girl opening the back door and saying, "How long am I supposed to let the spaghetti boil in that pan, Gwen?"

"Take a strand out and see if it's tender. If it is, then the spaghetti should be good."

"Sandy says I'll ruin it."

Gwen, her head angled so that she could see the pig-tailed girl, who looked to be twelve or so, said, "You'll do fine. You made bacon and eggs last Sunday and everybody liked them."

"Sandy says anybody can make bacon and eggs."

"Well, then next time we'll ask Sandy to do the Sunday breakfast after Mass and we'll see how well she does. How's that?"

"Can I tell her that?"

Gwen laughed. "I'm afraid it might come out mean, the way you'd say it. Better let me tell it."

"Okay," the girl said. But disappointment crimped her face. She'd obviously been hoping to torture Sandy with the bad news. She closed the door and was gone.

"You're quite the diplomat."

"So are you," Gwen said. "I'm still not sure why you're here."

"About a man named Earle Yancy."

The bright blue eyes showed anger. "I hope he wasn't a friend of yours."

"Nope. I barely knew him. And the first time I met him, I knocked him unconscious."

"Good. Somebody should've done that a long time ago. I know he's dead and that it isn't very Christian of me to say that."

"You really disliked him?"

"He was a terrible influence on some of the older boys."

"How so?"

"He got them to do what he called 'errands' for him." She steepled her pale hands out in front of her. A yellow cat walked up and positioned herself for a good long scratch. Gwen obliged. "A lot of these kids are what the newspapers call 'street urchins.' I hate that term but there isn't much I can do about it. Anyway, the four boys he dealt with had already been in some trouble with the law. So it wasn't hard for him to talk them into 'helping' him, as he called it."

"Helping him how?"

She showed plain disgust on her face. "Well, he got one of the boys to take one of our girls and put her on the street. She's very pretty. She became very profitable for Earle. Then he'd go drink at an expensive place and get a well-off man to get good and drunk, and then he'd have a couple of the boys rob the man when he left wherever he'd been drinking. There were burglaries, too. He taught them a lot of tricks. I'd never seen burglary tools before, but I found a set in one of the boys' bags. He was twelve years old at the time. He was teaching them how to be criminals is what it came down to. He'd rake off half the profits for himself — the boys told me all about this when I finally found out what was going on — and he had even bigger plans for the future." She paused. "But something happened three or four nights ago. One of the boys — an older one, seventeen — he came in very late and he was pretty bloody and battered. I took him out here so we could talk without waking the other kids. At first, he wouldn't tell me anything. Then all of a sudden, he started crying. You see that sometimes. They just break like that. They put on this tough act, but then it just doesn't work anymore and they break down. They're really scared little kids inside. Most of them, anyway. They're not angels. But they're not devils, either. Tim Mainwaring, the boy I'm talking about, he finally admitted that Earle had beaten him up pretty badly. Tim said he'd found something out that Earle didn't want him to know. Then he told me why Earle got so mad. It was really stupid."

"What got Earle so mad?"

She shook her head. "I guess for want of a better word, he tried to blackmail Earle."

"Blackmail him over what?"

"He wouldn't say. All he'd tell me is that he followed Earle somewhere and learned something. And then he said that he told Earle he wanted a hundred dollars or he'd tell somebody what he'd found out. He said he was afraid Earle was going to kill him. He only escaped because an old woman heard Earle beating him — Tim's very little and not tough at all — and she started screaming for Earle to leave Tim alone. Earle ran away. Tim said he was afraid Earle was going to find him and kill him."

"I'd like to talk to this Tim. Is that possible?"

"A few days ago it would have been."

"Why a few days ago?"

"He ran away in the middle of the night. I wouldn't be surprised if he hopped a freight. A couple of the boys lived on the rails for a while. They made it sound very romantic. Tim was always talking about how he wanted to be a hobo, too. Maybe that's what he did."

"Any chance he could be hiding in the city here?"

"A chance, sure."

"He have any particular friends here? Anybody he might have confided in?"

"Huh-uh."

"Huh-uh."

Those blue eyes watched me carefully. Maybe she thought I'd do or say something of significance that would tip her to who I was and what I really wanted.

"I don't think you're telling me the truth," I said.

"I'm not."

Now it was my turn to watch her carefully. If she hadn't started to irritate me, watching her would have been a pleasure.

"I'm lying to you because you're lying to me," she said.

"I haven't told you a single lie."

"Sins of omission and commission."

"I forgot. A Catholic girl."

"You won't tell me who you are, so I won't tell you what you want to know."

"You're a tough one."

"I have to be."

"Look," I said, "if I could tell you who I am, I would. But I can't. Don't you want to find Tim?"

"Of course. I've been saying prayers every half hour for him."

"Then help me. Let me talk to his friend. If I find Tim, I'll bring him back here and you can talk to him. Tell him he should be here instead of on the rails."

She reached down and scratched the patient cat, who'd been waiting for her second feast of human fingers. She finally picked her up and sat the cat in her lap. "You should've been an attorney."

"I wouldn't wish that on anybody."

"I don't like it that you won't tell me who you are. But I guess you're right. Maybe if you can get Brian to talk to you — well, he won't tell me anything. He's loyal to Tim. But maybe he'd talk to a man."

"That's all I want. Just to talk to him. Maybe it'll lead to Tim coming back here. Is this Brian here now?"

"No. He got himself a job working in a warehouse starting at three in the afternoon. He usually gets back here about ten. He's pretty dragged out then, too. I fix him something to eat and he goes straight to bed. He's a good kid." She smiled. "They all are. I didn't mean to slight any of them."

I was going through one of my little crushes. She'd be on my mind for at least a couple of hours, like the scent of a woman's perfume you savor until it fades.

"I'll be here around ten o'clock."

I didn't recognize him at first. He was out of uniform, in shirt and trousers only. He sat in one of the lobby chairs. He wasn't reading anything or even looking around. It wasn't hard to imagine what he was so intensely thinking about. His dead son Earle.

I went over and sat in the chair next to him. He didn't seem to know I was there until I spoke.

I said, "You look like you could use a drink."

His anger was instant. "You make it sound like we're friends, Mallory. We're not. And you'd damned well better remember that."

"Is there some way I can help you?"

"Don't give me that bullshit. You couldn't care less."

"Look, he was your son. I'm sorry for your loss, all right? I'm not pretending I cared much for him, but right now you look like hell and I'm sorry for that."

He glared at me. "You're a slick bastard."

"I wasn't trying to be slick, Yancy."

"You're also a liar."

"You're the second person who's called me that in the past hour."

"I just keep thinking about how you worked him over with your sap."

"I just keep thinking about how he worked over that girl with his fists."

He stood up without warning. Even in street clothes, he had that British look, that cropped gray hair, the severe little mustache, and the peerless ramrod posture. "Let's have that drink."

The taproom was getting crowded now that the businessmen were having drinks before heading home. There was a table near the back. We both ordered bourbon.

"I did some checking on Walter Tomkins," he said. "A couple of the men who served with me in the war ended up in Washington. One of them's in the Secret Service. I wired him."

"I don't suppose you'll be telling me his name."

"He wired me this afternoon, said that Tomkins worked in government and that from what he'd been able to gather it was some kind of organization that tracked financial problems. The whole thing is secret, he said. Technically, it doesn't even exist. Since I'm not stupid, Mallory, I assume this means that the President or somebody near him doesn't trust the standing organizations to do the job. He's probably afraid of corruption in his own ranks. They get close to big money, they get bought off or they start dipping into the till. I have the same problem as police chief. Probably a fourth of my men are on the take one way or another. Hard to prove and it's not worth going after because at this point it's still pretty minor." He knocked back some bourbon. "My guess is

210

that you work for the same folks Tomkins did. My other guess is that Earle figured into all this somehow."

"Interesting," I said.

"I didn't expect you to admit anything. All I give a damn about in this is finding who killed my son."

"I don't blame you."

"Maybe we could help each other."

"Maybe," I said. "I'd have to think about it."

He said, "There were so many things I wish we'd talked about. He was a smart kid, too smart, really, for his own good. I don't know why the hell he was so attracted to the wrong side of the street." No tears. No drama. Just a hard man puzzling through some hard thoughts. "You didn't need to use that sap on him the way you did, Mallory. I can't get it out of my mind."

"He might've killed me otherwise."

"I doubt that, Mallory." He got to his feet and then flung some clattering coins across the table. "You're too big of a prick to die."

He disappeared quickly into the noisy throng lining the bar.

FIVE

Natalie had slid a note beneath the door of my hotel room.

SEE YOU AT SIX. DIRE CONSEQUENCES IF YOU FORGET.

It had been a long time since I'd received a perfumed letter from a lady. Even standing there in my dusty and sweated clothes, my hair nearly white with the dust, the letter gave me a real boost. I guess you never get too old to feel young. It never lasts long, that almost-forgotten feeling of youth, but when it strikes you it sure is sweet. . . . For just a second there, I felt like I was seventeen again and squiring a lovely town girl around the Dartmouth campus. It felt damned good. My crush on Gwen had faded by this time. Your heart is as fickle as your crotch sometimes.

I had time for a long, hot bath and a short, sound nap before getting dressed and going down the hall to get Natalie.

She wasn't there.

At first, I thought she might be playing a joke on me. A little retribution for me not being with her last night. But by my fourth knock, I realized that it wasn't a joke. She really wasn't there.

The desk clerk told me that he'd seen her go out about an hour earlier. He said she looked upset. Didn't even respond to his greeting. And normally she was one of the friendliest guests they'd ever had.

I told him I'd be in the restaurant, waiting for her. He assured me he'd tell her the moment she crossed the threshold.

I ended up eating dinner alone. I wasn't mad, but I was worried. Natalie was one of those women who take duty and responsibility seriously. Look what she was doing for her brother. She could easily have walked away and forgotten him entirely. He was a pain in the ass and there wasn't anything in it for her except heartache. She had her own inheritance and to hell with him. But she'd never *say* to hell with him, and that's why I was uneasy about her not being here now.

I was back in my room by eight. I spent an hour on my report, catching up the past couple days. I planned to leave around nine-thirty to meet with Brian at the St. Christopher's Center.

The knock came just before nine. There was so much traffic in the hallway, I'd given up listening to footsteps shortly after I started working on the report.

The knock was curt, businesslike.

I grabbed my Colt, went to the door, opened it.

A middle-aged woman in a bonnet and aproned-dress stood there. "Are you Mr. Mallory?"

"Yes, ma'am, I am."

I kept tight hold of the gun in my right hand. I didn't point it at her, but I was ready to if necessary. There was a bland woman much like her who'd been a paid assassin during one of New Orleans's more corrupt periods, corruption, of course, being nearly unheard of there otherwise.

"The mister, he sent me here. He said to tell you she's very sick and wants to talk to you." She couldn't take her eyes from my Colt.

I relaxed a little. She was so nervous, I couldn't see her as an assassin. That takes some poise and self-confidence.

"I'm sorry if the gun scares you, ma'am. I won't hurt you. But you forgot to mention any names in what you said. Now, who sent you?"

"The mister. Mr. Kimble."

"All right. Who's sick?"

"The missus. Mrs. Kimble. I'm their housekeeper."

I try not to be cynical, but it's pretty damned hard in a world like ours. What if you wanted to set a trap for somebody? And what if, to set this trap, you sent an overwrought but obviously decent woman to summon your prey? Wouldn't your prey go along with the summons? That sweet middle-aged face and that nervous manner — who could doubt her?

Well, cynical as I was, *I* couldn't.

"Let me get my coat," I said.

PART FOUR
SERENA FAYE HOPKINS

Serena Hopkins and her first cousin Sam had been playmates since they were tykes, and around age seven they started taking painful, nervous interest in each other's private parts. She boldly asked Sam if she could watch him pee. He obliged her. Then it was her turn. She squatted down and did the deed. Sam didn't think this was fair because with her squatting down this way he couldn't see her privates. She didn't think it was fair that she had to squat because it looked so much easier to be standing while you did it.

Their first kiss was when they were eight. Afterward, at home in her mansion, Serena asked her mother if they, Serena and Sam, could ever get married.

"Lord, no, Serena," her mother, a proper woman, snapped. And then caught herself. She was talking to an eight-year-old who didn't understand the implications of her words. "You see, dear, you and Sam are first cousins. The Bible forbids first cousins from marrying and so does the law."

"But why?"

"Well, I'm not sure you're old enough to understand this yet, dear, but when it comes time to have babies — well, it's a matter of blood."

"Blood? What's blood got to do with it?"

Serena's mother laughed. "You're sure making this difficult for me, daughter. I'll tell you what. On your ninth birthday — which isn't that far away — I'll explain it all to you."

"My birthday isn't till winter and it's just spring."

"Time goes by so quickly, Serena. You'll see."

That night, just as she was going to sleep, Serena's mother wondered — Good Lord, why did she have to have thoughts like these? — if Serena and Sam ever . . . The mother had her own secrets in this regard. She'd twice let Billy Pemberton — they were then both eleven — put his hand between her legs so he could feel it. But he wasn't satisfied. He said he wanted to see it. He told her she wasn't a very good describer and that he just couldn't see his way to playing with her anymore — she was, after all, a girl, and he was a boy and should be out playing baseball anyway — then he just wouldn't come around anymore. She showed it to him twice. And then he never came around anymore.

Could Serena and Sam . . .

Serena grew to be the predominate beauty in her very upper-upper-class group of teens. Spoiled, vain, a cold and ruthless heartbreaker, she shocked everybody when, at twenty-one, she married a rich widower of forty-two and moved to his fortress in the mountains.

Sam, strapping, handsome, drunken, didn't have her good fortune. He drifted through jobs he found demeaning — actually, he found all jobs demeaning; he was one lazy sonofabitch — living mostly on an overly generous allowance provided — along with endless prayers that he straighten up — by his widowed mother. The recession of the late seventies changed that. His mother lost everything and was forced to move in with her rich sister and live very much like her sister's maid, said sister having never forgiven her for having larger breasts and prettier eyes.

Now Sam and Serena had never stopped seeing each other. Her husband wasn't much interested in sex. He wanted the same kind of housewifely affection he'd enjoyed with his first wife, a dutiful Methodist from Minnesota. He chose the wrong gal with Serena. She and Sam managed to meet three or four times a week. She often had to give him money to pay rent on the hovel he lived in. She also often had to remind him to bathe more frequently. But she'd never had a lover like Sam, and knew she never would. He didn't give a damn about contraception, but she did. While it was against the federal law to disseminate or distribute contraceptives through the mail or across the state lines, there was a woman often whispered of among the more daring Denver socialites . . . a woman who sold the latest in contraceptives made out of freshly slaughtered sheep intestines. . . .

Her husband had made his money in the short-haul train business. He was a sentimental family man. His two obnoxious daughters and their respective obnoxious broods were at the house frequently. Serena thought that anybody as dull as her husband just had to be stupid — i.e., he would never catch on to her trysts with Sam.

Well, he didn't, in fact, catch on. But one day — one of those terrible coincidences confused with fate and destiny — one of his ugly daughters happened to be boating with her husband and saw Sam and Serena strolling along the edge of the riverbank. The husband of the ugly daughter was an ugly attorney at law who quite often hired the services of the Pinkertons to help him in his defense of clients. The next time he was in the office, he hired a Pink to follow Serena starting immediately.

The predictable came true. At least the first half of it was predictable. Ugly daughter gathered evidence and presented it to naïve father. Naïve father confronted erotic wife and pleaded with her to change her ways. She promised, then two days later slept in a barn loft with Sam, a Pink standing on the wind side of said barn. Naïve husband scorns wife and orders her out of the house. Serena knew she would never see any of his money now. But what choice did she have? She packed two bags and left, the ugly daughter screeching at her all the time she packed. Whore. Slattern. Tart. Slut. She sure knew a lot of whore names for such a deeply pious ugly daughter.

That was the predictable part.

The unpredictable part came later that night when the naïve husband managed to find Sam. Naïve husband toted an ax. He chopped Sam into thirty-eight pieces and hurled the pieces into the river. He then went home and killed himself with his father's pistol.

Serena stayed in town and became the paramour of Arthur K. Davis, who kept her in luxury of a sort. He was not as wealthy as the naïve husband had been.

It was Davis that Vince Kelly contacted. It was also Davis that suggested Serena be used to seduce Henry Cummings in Washington, D.C. Unbeknownst to Davis, Kelly slept with Serena eight times just to make sure she was the kind of female he needed for this particular task. Not that Davis would have given that much of a damn even if he'd known. Unbeknownst to Serena, he had a mulatto girl he kept on the edge of the colored section. She was sweet and sexy. Serena was sour and sexy. Sour can wear a man down.

Serena was excited. She loved travel. And she loved entrapping men. Since Sam had died — my God, the nightmares she had about him being chopped up that way — she found men rather dull, actually, unless she wanted something from them they were at first unwilling to give — their bank account, their marriage, their heart. The fun was in taking these things without giving anything back but sex, which she put no value on since Sam was gone.

ONE

There was a white-haired man in a black suit helping himself to some brandy when the housekeeper brought me into Larry Kimble's den. The room was large but pretty much clichéd, right down to the massive globe, the bear and moose heads on the walls, and the floor-to-ceiling bookcase crammed with uniform editions of classics that nobody here had ever read.

The white-haired man had a face so wrinkled he looked like a walnut with eyes. He said, "You Mallory?"

"Yep."

"I'm Dr. Schulz. She's pretty sick. But she says she wants to talk to you."

"What's wrong with her?"

"Infection." He shrugged. He took a big chug of brandy and then tucked a thumb into a vest pocket. An enormous gold watch chain stretched across his girth. "That kills more pregnant women than anything else these days. Back East, they keep sayin' that they're developin' all these new drugs. But you know how they are

223

back East. I haven't seen any of those drugs yet. And neither has anybody else."

During my days as a would-be cowhand, I'd learned one thing about Westerners. They despised Eastern land barons, bankers, politicians, and professors on general principle. If it was East, it was automatically suspect. All you had to say around here was that somebody was from the East, and you could hear a lynch mob forming in the street. With the exception of the gentry, of course, who looked down on all things Western and filled their closets with Eastern clothes and their minds with Eastern thoughts.

"She going to make it?"

"Maybe."

"That doesn't sound very optimistic."

"You want the truth or you want pipe dreams?" His temper was as quick as mine.

Kimble came in, then. He looked pale, beaten.

"Damnit, Larry, have you eaten anything yet?"

"Not yet, Frank."

"Well, you have your housekeeper fix you something right now. Broth, if nothing else. And a piece of bread. This could be a long night."

Kimble said, "Thanks for coming, Mallory."

"I guess I'm still not sure why I'm here."

"All I know is that she wants to talk to you." Kimble said to the doctor, "You think you could leave us alone, Frank? I don't need to be rude."

"I need to look in on her, anyway. Then bring Mallory up. He'll only get a few minutes. She needs to sleep."

He grabbed his black leather bag and left.

"He's the best in the city," Kimble said.

I wondered if he was saying this for his sake or mine.

Now it was his turn at the brandy decanter. He raised it to see if I wanted any. I shook my head. I still wanted to be at St. Christopher's at ten. Sober.

He poured himself a small glass and said, "There's a good chance she's going to die." His eyes filled with tears. "I didn't want her to try to have a baby. It was just so risky."

"Your doctor says it's an infection. Doesn't sound like it's the pregnancy itself."

"Whatever it is." He gave a tiny sob. "Hell, I'm sorry. Crying like this."

"You love her."

He nodded, snuffling tears up. "You loved her, too, Mallory."

"For a long time. Yes."

"I think she knows she's dying. I think that's why she asked for you to come out. I think she wants to try and make amends. That's what she did with Kelly."

"He was here?"

"About an hour ago. He only spent five minutes with her. That's how sick she is. Then we had a talk. A good one. Kelly and I, I mean." Then: "I don't care about finding the plates or Cummings anymore. Obviously, neither does Cora. Even Kelly said he's thinking of moving on tomorrow. We had this whole thing in place — we were going to flood four states with Cummings's money; we were going to be so rich — and then somebody took him and his plates. After all that work Serena did in Washington — all the plans we made." He drained his drink. "This whole thing was cursed from the start. As soon as Kelly got rid of Mitch Michaels. Michaels was a lot smarter than the rest of us. Too smart in a lot of ways. But Kelly still shouldn't have killed him. Michaels had a family and everything."

"I almost forgot about him. When you say 'got rid' of him, what does that mean exactly?"

"I'm not sure. Mitch gave the impression of being very slippery. He was going to oversee the four people who passed the money. Kelly said we should pay him off and get rid of him."

"You think that's what happened?"

His knuckles went white on his glass. He was holding himself together through sheer will. His wife possibly dying, his bank certain to be taken from him once an audit was done. And if the district attorney didn't believe him, he could be facing jail. "You have to understand something. I'm not a criminal. I've never known people like Mitch or Kelly before in my life. Arthur Davis — well, his kind of man I *was* used to. He was like my former business partner. He played everything right up to the edge of legality. Then he got used to stepping one or two steps over the line. But he wasn't a professional like Mitch or Kelly."

I said it as gently as I could. "Or Cora."

He let out a long, sad sigh. "Yes, like Cora, too, I suppose.

"I always had this feeling about it, that we'd never pull it off. And now we won't." He poured himself more brandy. "You won't quit, though, will you?"

"Not until I get the plates and find out what happened to Cummings."

"Somebody killed Earle Yancy because he knew where Cummings was. That's what I'm thinking."

"I'm thinking that Henry Cummings is the one behind all these murders," I said.

His head jerked back and he looked at me. "B-by G-God, I n-never thought of that. My G-God."

I turned toward the door. "I'll go see Cora now."

The housekeeper led me down a long, carpeted hallway. The doctor was just opening a door and emerging. Bag in hand.

"She keeps getting weaker, Mallory. You won't have long. She has to rest."

I nodded and went inside.

It was hot the way sickrooms frequently are. There weren't any of the cancer smells, no rotting innards, no crusty flesh. Just medicine smells and sleep smells.

It was a large room with massive Victorian furniture, including a canopied bed and six-drawer bureau that reached my chest. Flickering lamplight gave her face a yellow cast. She must have been cold. The heavy covers were pulled near her neck. Her long, slender hands lay folded on top of the covers. The floor creaked once as I moved toward the bed. Her eyes opened.

She seemed to have difficulty smiling — as if she didn't quite have the strength — but then the smile came and the fine bones of her face were displayed to the full measure of art. She was classical beauty.

I leaned over and put my hand on hers. "I don't want you to talk. You need your strength."

"I had it all worked out. What I was going to say."

I lifted my hand and touched it to her fevered lips. "The past is past." I shrugged. "That's all there is *to* say."

Her eyelids fluttered. I wondered if she was starting to fade completely. "You ever figure out if you believed in an afterlife or not?"

"Nope. I've haven't figured that one out yet. Along with a lot of other things."

"I haven't figured it out yet, either." She was having some kind of pain or discomfort because she grimaced and gasped for a couple of seconds. "I'm going to pretend there is an afterlife, though. And I'm going to pretend that I'm going to heaven." A raspy little cough. "And I'm going to pretend you forgive me."

The grimace again. This time I realized what it was. The baby was kicking. Her eyes opened wide, those eyes I'd loved so long and so uselessly. "She's going to be beautiful. And she's going to be smart. And she's not going to make any of the mistakes I did, Dev."

"You didn't do so bad," I said. I knew now she was going to die. I wasn't sure what I felt or even what I should feel. It was probably going to be the way it was when my father died. I did all the ceremonial mourning but it took a couple of months — and for no particular reason at all — to miss him on a gut level. Then I just sat down and cried like a kid.

The doctor knocked once and came through the door. "It's time, Mallory," he staged-whispered.

I bent over and kissed her on the forehead. I was glad the doctor had come. I had no words left in me for her.

She collapsed into sleep even before I'd turned around. The doctor and I did everything in pantomime as he showed me out.

They were out in force, a part of big-city life whether the city was located in the East or West. The gangs. Even when you couldn't see them, you could hear them running in alley shadows and crouched behind trees and hiding ahead of you or behind you, trying to figure out if you were worth attacking and, if so, which was the approach of greatest advantage. I hadn't seen a one of them. You rarely did until it was too late. But you could hear them the way you could hear most nocturnal creatures. They'd learned the secret of urban invisibility. Most of them wouldn't have graduated to firearms yet — plus even holding a firearm could get you thrown in jail for a considerable amount of time — but who needed guns when you had knives, clubs, and socks filled with rocks. It was fine to pity them — I generally believed the arguments of the so-called "reformers" that most of these teens would have turned out all right if they'd had better childhoods — but pity them afterward, as a British wit had once remarked. When you were on a dark street and they were gathering in small feral packs to attack you — no pity then.

I suppose that's why I broke his arm.

Usually, they come at you in threes or even fours. Maybe this one was going through some kind of initiation ceremony. They're very big on initiation ceremonies. Show everybody how fearless and tough you are. Attack the man in the good suit all by yourself. Take him down, stomp him, rob him blind. Now you're a man.

The trouble with this approach is that occasionally you meet somebody who has an advantage you haven't anticipated. Walking along the shadowy street on my hurried way to St. Christopher's, I imagine I looked like any other businessman. Nobody to worry about, in other words. Probably going to a whorehouse. There were plenty of them in this neighborhood.

But here he came and I was ready for him.

He leapt on my back, deftly sliding his forearm around my throat, and doing a damned good job of cutting off my supply of air. Whoever had taught him, had taught him well. His throat-grip was strong enough to make my knees buckle. It wouldn't be long before I'd be on the ground and then they'd all be swarming on me, fresh meat.

He'd surprised me with his choke hold.

I surprised him right back by grabbing his arm at the elbow and giving it a twist forceful enough to break bone. His scream probably woke four square blocks of sleepers.

Then I had my Colt out and pressed the barrel to his head. In the faint moonlight, my attacker appeared to be thirteen or fourteen. But the way he was sobbing, he sounded more like six or seven. Any pity I might have felt for him vanished when a butcher knife fell from his other hand. The blade glinted in the light.

A towheaded kid said, "He never done this before, mister. He got scared. He don't know how to do it right yet."

"You ever think maybe he shouldn't have been doing it at all?"

There were four of them. Two Mexicans and two whites. One of the whites was fifteen or so and had a ragged scar across his forehead, as if somebody had slammed the edge of a shovel blade into him. He said, "I think you broke his arm, mister."

The attacker continued to sob and hold his broken arm tenderly.

I shoved him toward his friends.

"I did break his arm. He deserved it." I leveled my Colt at one of the Mexicans and said, "You look like the oldest. You better tell the young ones they can get killed doing this. They probably think it's fun. But that one sure isn't having any fun now."

"Aw, shit; aw, God; aw, fuck," the attacker was saying over and over again, rocking his entire body back and forth, as if the pain could be lessened by movement.

I holstered my Colt.

They grabbed the noisy attacker and scurried away into the gloom.

No lights in the second-floor window; only a front room light on the ground floor. No noises, either. St. Christopher's was buttoned up for the evening.

Gwen answered on my first knock. "Hi."

As she led me to the kitchen, I saw kids everywhere on the floor. Tucked beneath blankets. Sleeping. Snoring. Muttering dream words. We moved on tiptoes and didn't speak. The kitchen had a door you could close. She closed it. I smelled coffee.

"That smells good," I said.

"That a hint?"

"More like a plea. I may have a long night ahead of me."

"You looked a little mussed."

"Ran into some old friends of mine in a street gang."

"Oh, Lord. Really?"

"Afraid so."

She wrapped her hands around the coffee cup, as if trying to get warm. "They were raised like animals, a lot of them, so I feel sorry for them. But they still have to take responsibility for what they do. I'm sort of in the middle of the whole argument about street gangs. Some people just want to throw them in adult prison and forget about them. And other people basically don't want to hold them accountable for anything. I don't agree with either side. I think we should try to help them all we can, but if they hurt somebody, then they should be punished the way anybody else would."

"I may've gone a little overboard tonight." I told her about breaking the kid's arm.

Her expression changed subtly. The jaw muscles bunched at the hinges; a distinct displeasure shone in her dark eyes. "I sensed violence in you. Maybe a lot of violence."

"I don't think of myself that way. I just try to survive is all. He was strong enough to have killed me."

"You could've just thrown him off you."

"True."

"But you decided to really hurt him."

"Maybe I was trying to teach him a lesson."

"You don't really believe that, do you?"

I shrugged. "No, I guess I don't. I got a little scared and I got a little mad when he was choking me. I wanted to hurt him back. Maybe it's that simple."

That long, somber face lifted, the blue eyes narrowing. Her head tilted to the right. She was listening to the front door open. I'd heard feet on the front stoop moments earlier.

"Brian?" I said.

"Maybe."

In a minute he was there, standing just inside the closed kitchen door. My back was to him when he came in so he spoke first to Gwen.

"Brian, this is Mr. Mallory. He'd like to talk to you about Tim."

I shifted around in my chair. We both got the same kind of jolt at the same time. He was the gang member with the jagged scar across his forehead. I was the man who'd broken his young friend's arm.

He gave a little start and then said, "Hi."

"Hi, Brian."

I put out my hand. We shook. He was clearly afraid I was going to rat him out. I was happy to let him think that for right now. It would keep him off balance.

"Brian, Mr. Mallory would like to talk to you about Tim."

"I don't know nothing about him," Brian said. "He took off is all I know." He didn't have a tough face, just a sullen one. He wore a frayed gray work shirt and jeans. The forehead scar was impressively nasty in good light.

Gwen stood up. "I need to check on some things upstairs. You two can talk down here."

"Thanks, Gwen," I said.

"You be nice, Brian. Help him all you can."

"I don't know anything. I told you." His voice was now as sullen as his face.

"Well, do your best."

After she left, Brian said, "You didn't need to break his fucking arm."

"I probably didn't. But then you didn't need to be preying on every helpless sonofabitch who was walking the streets tonight, either. And anyway, Gwen seems to think that you were at work tonight."

He came over and sat in Gwen's chair and said, "Mr. Bishop fired me two weeks ago. Me'n this other kid got into a fight on the loading dock. He said I took this comb of his. He's always combin' his hair with it. He's like a girl when he gets that damned comb in his hand. Everybody likes him except me. He's pretty tough. He was always pushin' me around. He was ridin' my ass all night about this stupid comb. I didn't know anything about it. I didn't think it was about the comb, anyway. We all had this picnic one Sunday. I think his girl-friend kind of liked me. She kinda hung around me most of the time. He didn't like that. I tried to stay away from her 'cause I knew what he'd do to me. He just bided his time, I guess, and came up with this comb thing. He started shoving me when we were out on the dock that night. Mr. Bishop, he forgot something at the office so he came back late. He got there just when I shoved Ned into a wall. He'd been shovin' me all night. I was just payin' him back. Well, so Mr. Bishop sees this and he thinks I'm the instigator of the whole thing. So he fires me. Ned, he doesn't do nothin' to. *Me* he fires. Nobody'd take my part because they're all afraid of Ned."

"That doesn't explain why you were with the street gang tonight."

He picked up Gwen's coffee cup and took a drink from it. "She don't mind."

"So why were you with the gang tonight?"

"I used to run with them before I came here, to St. Christopher's. I was afraid to tell Gwen I got fired. She was the one who got me the job and all. She's such a good woman, you wouldn't believe it. Anyway, I had to go somewhere at night so Gwen'd think I was working, so . . . well, I just went and saw the old gang again. They were happy to see me back. I used to be pretty good at pickin' locks and things. We broke into a lot of places when I was around ten or so."

"You glad to be back with them?"

He shook his head. "I guess not. I — it gets kind've scary sometimes."

"Good. Being scared is good. It's one way of learning common sense." I watched him drink more of Gwen's coffee. "I need to find Tim."

"I don't know where he is."

"You're lying."

"Hey. I don't have to take any shit from you."

"Sure you do. Because if you don't, I go to the police and tell them that you were part of a gang that tried to rob me. Then they'll give you the choice of going to jail or turning on your gang. Personally, I'd take jail over facing up to some of the boys in your gang."

"He ran away."

"To where?"

"He didn't say."

"He's still here, in town, isn't he?"

"No."

"He's still here, isn't he?" I repeated.

"I don't have to answer your question."

"We've been through this one. Sure you have to answer my question. Now where is he?" Then I told him how much I'd pay him. It was enough to make his head snap up.

"Is that true?"

"It's true. Plus you don't have to rat out your gang or go to jail. But if you lie to me, I'll come after you. You saw what I did to the new recruit. I'll do worse to you."

He stared at me. "I don't really like you."

I stared back. "I don't really care."

"Cops're nicer than you are."

"Not all cops. I could introduce you to a few who'd make you hide under your bed. They scare the hell out of me, anyway."

"When would I get this money?"

"You wouldn't get it."

"You just said —"

"The money would go to Gwen. She can give it to you a little at a time. You take it out on the street, that gang of yours will take it."

Without pausing, he said, "No, they wouldn't." Then he thought it over: "Well, I guess they might."

"You trust Gwen, right?"

"Of course. Everybody in the center does."

"Then you know your money is safe."

"I guess that's true."

I put a cigarette in my mouth and said, "Where is he, Brian?"

"I think he's in that house above the river."

"What house above the river?"

He described location and house. Then: "There's a real small limestone pit behind it."

"Why do you think he's there?"

"It's just a guess."

"He tell you he might go there?"

"No. But he got real excited about it. He was doing something for Earle one night — Earle wanted him to burn down this barn of this farmer who owed Earle money and wouldn't pay him — anyway, so he swings back toward town and then he sees this house. Tim's this real good burglar. He can get into any house you name."

"Lot of men in prison you could say the same about."

"I guess that's true. But he really is good."

"So he breaks into the house —"

"He breaks into the house," he said, "and he can't believe what he sees."

Then he stopped talking.

"That's the end of the story, Brian?"

"Yeah. That's why I was so mad about it. He wouldn't tell me anything more about it. Except Earle had something to do with it, with the house I mean. That much he told me. He said he heard Earle talking about it with somebody one night. And that after he saw the house, he knew Earle would give him plenty of money not to tell anybody else about that house."

"Then Earle came after him."

"Yeah. I really think Earle wanted to kill him."

"So Tim pretended to run away."

"I think he really was gonna run away."

"What stopped him?"

"When Earle got killed. I was meeting Tim under this trestle bridge every night. He had money. He had a lot of money, in fact. He gave me some for myself and then had me buy him food and tobacco. Things like that. This was after I got fired, so I needed the money."

"You see him tonight?"

"No. He wasn't there last night. And he wasn't tonight. That's why I think he's in that house. He was so excited about — about whatever was in there. He almost acted crazy."

"You have any of the money he gave you?"

"Some, why?"

"I'd like to see it."

"See it? It's just plain, normal money."

"And you're sure it's the money he gave you?"

"I'm one-hundred-percent positive."

"Could I see some of it?"

"You going to give it back?"

"I'll answer that after I see it."

"What's that supposed to mean?"

I shoved my hand, palm up, to the middle of the table. "Let me see some of the money, Brian."

"Don't tell Gwen I've got it, all right?"

"All right."

"Promise?"

"Promise."

He laid some crimped paper money in my palm. I took it and worked on getting it to lie flat. "Bring that lamp over here, would you?" I asked him.

After I had better light, I started a careful examination of the money.

"What're you looking for?"

"Quiet. I'm trying to concentrate."

"But —"

"Quiet."

It wasn't as good as the paper money I'd seen in the Boss's office, but it was damned good. Except for the almost hidden smudges on the serifs of the words "Trust" and "Nation" on the backside of the bill.

"You find something?"

"I can't say. But I'll tell you what. I'll swap you this money for some of my own."

"The same amount?"

"You'll pick up ten percent more than you're giving me."

"Who wouldn't do that?"

"Good. Now I'll need directions from you to get to that house. Is that fair?"

Gwen sat on the stoop. I sat down beside her. Sounds in the night: saloons, factories, talk and laughter from different tenements on either side of the center. Sight: a vivid half-moon, a dog drinking from a puddle in the street, Gwen biting on a fingernail.

"That's supposed to give you appendicitis," I said.

"I'm worth my weight in fingernails. Anyway, I don't believe that about appendicitis. If that was true, I would've gotten it a long time ago."

"You always been a nail-biter?"

"I was probably a nail-biter in the womb."

"You seem so calm."

"Acting. Sometimes, I go into a room by myself and just tremble. Really shake, I mean. You ever do that? Tremble and shake like you're going to fly apart?"

"In the war I did that. Whenever I saw dead soldiers whose faces had been mutilated."

"Oh, Lord. I guess I've tried to forget about that. The Confederates were pretty bloody."

"We did it, too."

"You're kidding. Our side? Really?"

"Really."

She let out a long sigh. "The things people do to each other can really get me down. I see people who beat little kids — three- and four-year-olds — with belts and it's hard to think of them as even being human."

"Yeah, I get like that sometimes, too. That's why I could never be a lawman. On the wrong night, I might take the belt from the guy and beat him to death with it."

She gave a little laugh. "Well, you're certainly fun to hang around with, Mr. Mallory. You have any more mutilation stories you'd care to share?"

"Not only more stories. I've got photographs."

"I'll bet you have. So — and I'm definitely changing the subject here — was Brian any help?"

"He was, yes. Thanks for introducing me."

"I don't suppose you'd care to tell me what he said?"

"I promised him I wouldn't."

"Can you at least tell me if Tim is at least still in town?"

"Maybe."

"Is that a straight answer?"

"Straight answer. Brian isn't sure about that."

"If you find Tim, will you send him back?"

"I'll do my best."

"Maybe he won't want to come back. Maybe he'll go on the rails. . . ."

"That's a rough life. And a dirty one. Lots of real predators on the rails. Killers, perverts, lunatics."

"That sounds like one of my family reunions."

I smiled. "Remember to invite me next time you have one."

When I stood up, I stretched and yawned. "Well, I need to get some sleep tonight."

She stood up, brushed her bottom off with delicate fingers. I would have been happy to do it for her.

She said, "Tell him I'm worried about him. Tell him if he doesn't want to come back now, he can come back any time he wants to."

I kissed her on the cheek. Much as I wished I could have brushed off her bottom for her, my basic feeling toward her was that she was the sister I'd never had. Part woman, part idealistic kid, and damned good female. She *sure* didn't mind hard work.

"Well, that was a surprise," she said.

"Yeah, for me, too."

I started walking away.

"Please remember to tell him he can come back any time."

I waved without turning around. "That's the first thing I'll tell him."

Then I disappeared into the darkness.

There was a crowd outside my hotel. There was also a mortuary wagon and maybe half-a-dozen coppers in uniform and caps. There was the kind of excitement that only a death can produce. Fascination and fear mixed together into a heady brew. Sex is always good after a close-up gander at the man in the dusty robes, the one with that long merciless scythe in his hand. The old bastard doesn't care who he takes — some poor little tyke with whooping cough or some old drunken fall-down bum taking a leak behind a saloon — he just needs to stuff another soul or two into that burlap bag he drags behind him.

Chief Yancy was talking to a tall, spare man I suspected was the mayor. I'd seen a mayoral photograph in the paper. This appeared to be the same fellow. Yancy excused himself and walked over to me.

"I'm surprised to see you here," he said.

"Oh? This is where I'm staying. Why should that surprise you?"

He was in uniform, the natty little British officer with the natty little mustache out of the Rudyard Kipling story.

"Are you going to tell me that you were out tonight and are just now coming back to your room?"

"A mind reader," I said. "In fact, that's just what I *am* going to tell you."

A soft wind from the mountains. I'd leave the window open a few inches. Good sleeping weather, all warm beneath the covers.

"You have any particular reason for killing him?"

"You've got me at a disadvantage, Chief. I don't even know who you're talking about."

"Of course you don't. Man is in your hotel room, place stinks of whiskey. Man is shot twice in the chest, probably dead almost right away. Now he's sprawled in a chair, just about ready to fall off and hit the floor by the look of things. You want to go up and see him?"

"Now who'd pass up a chance to see something like that? Not me. I love being around corpses. By the way, do I get to know who the guy is?"

"Was," he said. "Was."

"Pardon my grammar. So who the hell was he, Yancy?"

Yancy smiled. "You're trying to shit a shitter again, Mallory. But I'll play along for now. I found out his real name from a wanted poster the other day. He was using Ted Nealon, but his real name was Vince Kelly."

Two

Shot twice in the chest. Killer apparently came in and exited through the window, taking full advantage of the wooden fire escape, which, when you think about it, doesn't make a hell of a lot of sense. The fire escape would likely burn right along with everything else.

But there were other matters at hand to worry about, weren't there?

What had Kelly been doing in my room? How had the killer known he was here? Who had killed him?

The first two, as I explained to the considerably cynical Yancy, were easy enough to answer. "Kelly wanted to tell me something. The killer had been following him for some reason. The killer takes the fire escape and climbs in here. If he even came in. I remember leaving the window partially open. The killer could have fired through the window. Two shots to the chest. And then the killer runs away."

We were in the room together. He'd told the other coppers to stay in the hall.

"The killer wasn't you, of course."

"Of course."

"So you wouldn't have any trouble finding people who would claim to have been with you the past hour and a half?"

"In fact, I have a whole gang of people who could alibi me. No thanks to your police force, a gang came after me just about ninety minutes ago."

"Bad section of town?"

"I suppose."

"You should've known better."

"That's reassuring. I like dynamic chiefs."

"We're wasting time, Mallory. Why was he in your room?"

"Just a friendly sort of fella, I guess."

"You're awfully chipper for somebody with a dead man in his room."

He went over to the window. While he was looking out, he took out a package of British cigarettes and lit one up.

"Anybody ever tell you those smell like skunk?" I said.

"You'll have to kill people more often, Mallory. It seems to put you in a good mood." He turned from the window and glared at me. "I asked you to cooperate the other day. Work with me. I take it you've decided against that."

"That would seem to be the case."

"You may be next. I assume you realize that. First Arthur Davis — which I've now decided wasn't an accident — then my son. And now this man." He kicked the bottom of Kelly's boot sole. "Something ties you all together. I'm not sure what yet. I just know that you all seem to be paying a high price for it."

I said nothing.

He took a drag off his fancy cigarette and said, "All I want is the person who killed Earle."

I dropped my patter. "If and when I find him, he's yours."

"I might kill him on the spot."

"I wouldn't try and stop you, if that's what you're worried about. And I wouldn't turn you in. If he was my son, I'd do the same."

He nodded. "Maybe you're not as big a shit as I thought."

"Careful now, Yancy. You're getting downright sentimental."

He laughed. "You can go now. You'll have to get a different room for tonight."

"Yeah," I said, "pretty soon he'll be getting ripe."

I slept in a tiny room on the first floor. It was near the back door, which was apparently the preferred entrance for drunks. I got to hear some singing, some pissing, some puking, some arguing, and some bouncing off walls in an attempt to stand upright.

I woke up without the help of a rooster shortly after dawn. I got a basin of fresh water, washed myself well, shaved, and put on clean clothes. No suit this time. Chambray shirt, jeans, and a special pair of boots. Each boot had a built-in scabbard that held a knife. I know that sounds awfully European, but the knife came in handy once when I sawed off the ear of a man who was going to blow up a train car. We had about forty-five minutes before said train car was going to blow. I thought maybe cleaving his ear off might impress upon him the urgency of the situation. The last thing I put on was my holster and Colt.

I packed each boot with a knife, found the only nearby café that was open already, ate a breakfast of easy-over eggs that proved to be even tougher than the small piece of steak that came with it, and then walked down to visit my old friends at the livery. I got the same horse I'd been riding the past few days. He didn't seem all that happy to see me, but I figured maybe six a.m. wasn't his favorite time of day. It sure wasn't mine.

The ride took nearly an hour. The countryside was a revelation of summer colors, early morning shadows, animals as friendly-looking as illustrations in children's books, and that tug of nature that makes even a city slicker like me learn how to cook various rocks and pieces of tree bark for sustenance and how to yodel in such a way that deer, moose, and elk become my lifelong friends.

The house was a Queen Anne in style. Or so the folks at Sears wanted you to believe it was, anyway. It was one of those homes you could order from the catalog and pound, stomp, and glue together yourself after it arrived. The white picket fence gave it a homey feel, the flowers along the front porch added color, and the frilly curtains on the front windows lent it a female air that was downright friendly.

But there was something wrong. That was as good as my warning system ever gets. It never tells me *what* is wrong. It just tells me that somewhere lurking in that little house is something that will do me harm. Maybe even great harm. Now maybe this could be somebody with a gun, or a rattlesnake coiled just inside the door, or a rabid dog in fevered need of a juicy section of flesh to sink its teeth into — the species doesn't matter. Squirrel, possum, copper, it is not particular.

I was happy I was toting my Colt and my twin knives.

I dropped off my horse and drew my Colt. I squinted into the sun. I couldn't see any evidence of a gun being held on me, though this might be because the sun was damned near blinding me at the moment.

I didn't go to the gate in front of me. Instead, I walked around the outside of the fence to the back. There was a rear exit. I didn't know if that was a good thing or not. If somebody was inside and was going to escape, this would be the logical door to use. If I was coming in the front way. If I was coming in the back way — you get the idea. I didn't know what the hell way to go in. The silent house offered not a single clue.

I walked back ten yards and took a look at the shallow limestone dig. I could see Earle Yancy hiding down there, maybe so drunk he rumbled all the way down in it, getting all dusty as he watched the house. Then he'd come to the boardinghouse, the way the landlady had described to me.

I walked around some more. If there was somebody in there, they might do me a favor by firing on me. At least, that way I'd know what I was up against. On the other hand, they might put a bullet in my brain and kill me. I had to read some of those dime novels. Those boys never had moments of indecision like this. They just charged blindly ahead and everything always worked out well for them, at least eventually. Sure, they had to escape the clutches of a few cannibal tribes, a few alligator pits, and moving walls that meant to crush you between them — but that didn't deter them a bit.

I stood next to my horse. The sun was starting to get warm. My horse dropped a couple of green road apples. A blue jay sat on the crown of my horse's head. A black fly kept diving at my hat. A possum skulked its way through the short grass, stopping about ten feet away to get a better look at the intruder, me. This was the world I rarely saw. The world of nature. God's world. To be honest, fascinating though it was, I would have preferred to be sitting in a sidewalk café in New Orleans or some such place, ogling ladies half my age and ripe with feminine splendor. My horse unloaded some more and the fly had a go at my nose.

I went inside. I'd rather be shot to death than bored to death.

My boots were loud on the porch. The house was in good repair. The paint was new, the carpentry was done well, and the porch felt sturdy.

I took out my burglary tools. What I was dealing with was a seemingly simple padlock that turned out to be not simple at all. It was brass with three tumblers and one of those new spring guards that cover the opening when the key is withdrawn. If you're working with a tool instead of a key, the spring guard tends to close early. In other words, it presses against the pick and makes working more difficult.

I had to spend around twelve minutes with it. Most other kinds of locks, I would have been inside in five or six minutes. If that.

The house was smaller inside than I'd expected, mostly because it had way too much furniture. The living room alone held a large horsehair couch, an oil stove, an upright piano, and a porcelain-lined bathtub. I assumed the latter was here because there was no other place to put it. The dining room included a mahogany table, four chairs, a glass-faced cabinet for good dishes, and three bookcases. Again, I had the sense that the bookcases were here because there was no other place to put them. I glanced at the titles. What a mix it was. Twain, H. Rider Haggard, Horatio Alger, Louisa May Alcott.

There were two framed photographs standing on a small table. Easy to see they'd been taken in Washington, D.C. Easy to guess that the man in them was Henry Cummings and that the woman and the two nearly grown daughters were his family.

The air was rich with the odors of recently cooked food — which I suspected had been cooked on the stove in the living room — tobacco, whiskey, and another scent that I didn't recognize at first.

The dining room had only one small window. I glanced into the living room and the gleaming stream of sunlight that touched the couch.

On my first look around, I'd missed the envelope on the floor next to the horsehair couch. Nothing special about it. A white business envelope. Looked as if it had just fallen there.

I picked it up, looked inside. Four one-hundred-dollar bills. I wasn't surprised by what I saw. After all, this was the point of the whole assignment, queer money. I took one of the bills to the window for a quick inspection. When I held it up to the stream of sunlight, it was easy to see the paper flaws, minuscule though they were. They wouldn't have any trouble passing this.

I stuck the envelope in my pocket and went on to the kitchen. The layout was impressive. What Cummings, or somebody, had duplicated here was a version of the layout you found in the Bureau of Printing and Engraving, right down to the same style of press. There were four worktables covered with inks, dyes, paper samples, watermarking implements, and God alone knows what else. In the east corner, I found eight heavy boxes of paper that had been shipped to Denver from a paper mill in Maryland. I opened one of the boxes and took out a sample. It wasn't the real thing, but it sure came close to duplicating the paper used by Uncle when he makes money. I kept rubbing it between thumb and forefinger. Sure felt true, too.

I walked over to the press, smelled it. Fresh ink. There was a box where they'd thrown away their press samples getting set up for the run. I fished a couple of them out. Hundred-dollar bills. You could see where the press operator had had to make adjustments. This was work that had to be *exactly* right, at least to the naked and bankerly eye. Even with the flaws of the samples — too heavily inked on one corner on one sample, canted to the right on another — the fake was damned convincing. I'd seen some really good stuff in my years with the company, but nothing that ever came close to this. Of course, Henry Cummings had brought the real thing to the table. The paper they were using was more than adequate — you'd have to know the details of the watermarking Washington uses to spot the paper as bum — and with the real plates and denominations of a hundred dollars . . .

It wasn't impossible to imagine Kelly and company spreading out in the states they'd designated, dispensing the million dollars that was their goal. . . . That's how it had happened a few years back, when some of the great creative criminal minds of our time (as the tabloids like to call them) got together to take advantage of a new process called photolithography, which allowed the crooks to briefly pass off nearly five million dollars. The usefulness of the process was short-lived, however. Good as the process was, some of the lines on the bills tended to blanch out. Bankers caught on fast. Misstep that it was, the boys — most of them in prison with little else to do — caught on to the uses of photoengraving. Now here was a method that was damned near foolproof in reproducing details on a bill. . . .

What I wanted, of course, were the plates. And what I didn't find, of course, were the plates.

There was one place I hadn't checked. The back porch. It was enclosed, so I hadn't been able to see anything from the backyard when I'd made my sweep.

I hadn't opened the door more than half an inch when the odor assaulted me. An unmistakable odor, it is. You smell it once, you never forget it. I'd found a couple Rebs, or their remains anyway, in a subbasement where somebody had shot them. They must have been there two weeks when I found them.

This stench was every bit as bad.

I took out a handkerchief and covered my face. They could at least have buried him.

For some reason, rats hadn't yet found him. The maggots had, of course. They looked like a giant moving scab. There was just enough left of his face so that I could identify him as Henry Stillman Cummings.

The same man in the photos in the front of the house. There were two bullet-sized holes in his forehead. One eye had been eaten away entirely. The other was only half-gone. He wore a peculiar grin or what looked to be a grin. I think it was probably not a grin at all, but simply the angle of his upper lip. A lot of it had been eaten away.

I was pretty sure that the teen sprawled in the corner, who had been even more viciously set upon by rats, was what had once been the missing boy from the St. Christopher's Center.

I searched the porch and found exactly what I assumed I'd find, which was absolutely nothing.

I went back to the kitchen and checked everything there again, too. Every drawer, every waste basket, every shelf. I didn't find anything I hadn't seen before. I'd taken all the receipts from the various supplies of paper, ink, and watermarking devices. When I did my final report, I'd paper-clip all these to the front of the document. A couple of these boys would be getting visits from someone in the Boss's office.

The smell of Cummings's body wouldn't leave my nostrils. I felt coated with invisible slime. I knew what it was. Though I'd mostly worked counterfeiting during the war, I'd had my share of narrow escapes. And my share of fighting. I'd seen and smelled corpses of every size, color, and description. Some soldiers had nightmares about these sights. It was funny, my problems with the dead usually came when I was awake. It was that corpse smell. I'd go a little crazy sometimes with fear. Death doesn't scare me particularly. But the dying it takes to get there sure has a way of unmanning me when I have to face it.

At this point, the stench got to me bad. I kicked out the back door — I didn't want to bother unlocking it — and stumbled outside. I was like a frantic man who'd almost drowned. Wanted to suffuse my entire body and soul with fresh air and sunlight and life. I did not want to die, not ever, I did not want to think about maggot-eaten faces or dirt-piled graves waiting to be filled or the cold eternal nothingness of extinction.

I wanted to run around dancing, run around singing, run around fucking my brains out. I wanted the word that our old Episcopalian parson always used, "Affirmation." I wanted to affirm my ass off.

It was panic, of course. I couldn't shake it. In the war I saw men, strong men, overloaded with dying and death, who'd go crazy for a time with panic. I was having another of my delayed reactions.

I rolled myself a cigarette and went and sat on a tree stump. Who the hell was killing all these people? The killings weren't necessary. Take the plates and run. None of the people in the counterfeiting ring, except possibly Vince Kelly, would ever have the skill to find the thief. So kill Kelly and leave the others alone. Could the killings be unrelated to the counterfeit? I didn't see how. You get some pretty strange coincidences in some cases, but I didn't see any way that could be possible in this case. Killings and counterfeit were related — but why and how?

I was happy to head back to Denver.

PART FIVE
HARVENIA SARA WAYLAND

Now, Harvenia had never heard of a long-ago man named Plato nor his theory that the uterus was this little animal inside the female body that would sometimes get restless and climb around inside the female and prove mighty uncomfortable. Mr. Plato further believed that the only thing that could make the animal lie down and rest was to bring the female to orgasm. Proving that not even geniuses could always be right.

By the time Harvenia came to be a midwife in the Denver area, Plato's idea of an "animal" had long been forgotten. But not the orgasm part. Doctors believed that when women got "hysterical" in any way, the only way to deal with it was to massage the clitoris. Doctors found this to be tiring and boring work, however, so they often hired women to do it. Harvenia was one of the midwives who found that massaging the clitoris helped during the birthing process. Orgasm didn't calm the mother entirely — she was, after all, undergoing a great deal of pain — but the orgasm often took the worst of the edge away.

This was a peripheral part of Harvenia's duties, of course, but one that was appreciated by many women because doctors just wouldn't do it. They had too many other appointments to get to.

Harvenia was an especially good midwife. In a time when as many as twenty percent of mothers were lost to infection, only one of her mothers had died and she'd delivered more than a hundred babies. There were four women physicians in Denver and Harvenia had paid calls on all of them, learning how to improve her skills and learning, equally important, to deal with this new concept of "germs." Current medicine believed that it was germs that infected and killed mothers and babies alike at the fragile time of birth.

Several months before her due date, Cora had started to ask women she knew who would be the best person to help her when her baby was born. She was surprised to find that most doctors, male and female alike, weren't much interested in childbirth. They frequently referred the women to a list of five midwives in whom they had absolute faith. Harvenia was always at the top of that list.

ONE

"Who killed him?"

"Wouldn't know."

"And what were you doing out there in the first place?"

"Just riding around. Saw the house."

"And being neighborly, you just dropped in."

"Pretty much."

"You sure run into a lot of corpses, Mallory."

"I could say the same for you."

"I have an excuse. I'm the chief of police."

About what I expected, sitting in his office with the door closed and talking to Yancy. We had our roles and we were pretty comfortable with them by now. The first thing I did after taking my horse back to the livery was wire the Boss and tell him about Cummings.

Now I had to sort of tell Yancy the truth. Some of it, anyway, now that I could be pretty sure he wasn't involved in any of it.

"When you ride out there, Chief, you'll

find a printing press and a lot of the things needed to make counterfeit money."

"Damn," he said.

" 'Damn?' "

"I thought I had some pretty good guesses in mind. But I didn't think about counterfeiting."

"That's what it's all about. My name really is Devlin Mallory. I work out of Washington, D.C., for the government. If you want to check me out here's a business card. You can wire this man and he'll tell you that I work for him, which I do."

"What's the name of the agency you work for?"

"It's a fake name and it doesn't matter, anyway. The only person I report to is the man whose name I just gave you. And the only man he reports to is the President's Chief of Staff. And once in a while, he sees the President himself. Though not very often."

"Well, I'll be damned." Then: "Do I get all the names of everyone around here who was involved in this operation?"

"As soon as I'm leaving, I'll tell you. Right now, they're the only people who can possibly lead me to the plates."

"Plates?"

I told him about Henry Cummings and

what he'd done in Washington and how —
this was my assumption now, anyway —
he'd been seduced into coming out here.

"Why all the way out here?"

"I'm not sure other than the fact that
there's been a lot of counterfeiting back
East and the Secret Service is all over the
place shutting down the various operations. The queer money printed out here
has usually been of poor quality. It gets
picked off right away by bankers and local
law. I suppose the kidnappers felt more
comfortable with the fact that out here,
there're no Secret Service people combing
the banks."

"I guess that makes sense. Now, one
more question."

"That one I don't have an answer for."

"My son is murdered. Davis is murdered. Kelly is murdered."

"And I don't know why any of them
were killed."

"Were any of them involved in the
counterfeiting?"

"I can't tell you that, Chief. When I
leave I'll fill you in on everything."

"Now I know that at least one of them
was."

I took a deep drag off my cigarette.
"You'll just have to assume what you want

to assume, Chief. I wish I could help you, but I can't."

I checked the clock tocking on his west wall. "Now I've got some other business."

"I could always have you followed."

"Yes, you could. But if you did, I could always get pissed off and not tell you everything you want to know when the time comes."

I stood up. So did he.

"I still want the person who killed my boy."

"You'll get him if you have a little patience. Then he'll be all yours."

Those hard blue eyes got even harder. "I'd appreciate that, Mallory. I really would."

She had a window seat in the hotel restaurant. At first, I didn't recognize her because of her outfit. The black dress was too big for her and the veil hid her face. My first impression, when she got my attention by knocking on the window, was that this was a woman in mourning. Then she lifted the veil, smiled grimly, and pointed to her black eye. It was quite the shiner.

After I was seated across from her, after I'd rolled and lighted a cigarette, after the waiter had brought me my life-force coffee, I said, "How does the other fella look?"

"He's in the hospital."

"Are you joking?"

"No. I'm not. A hospital for the insane."

"Your brother?"

"Exactly." She reached across the table, touched my hand. "I'm sorry about last night."

"Obviously, you had more important things to tend to."

"I'd agreed to meet him at his lawyer's office in the late afternoon. Well, the lawyer hadn't gotten back from the jail yet. There was some confusion about bail for a client of his and it took forever to get straightened out. Leaving me and my brother alone in the lawyer's office."

"Drunk?"

"No. And that's the funny thing. He actually held me and kissed me on the cheek when I got in there. And he was fine for about the first fifteen minutes. He said he'd decided that I was right, that he'd probably just spend or lose all his money, that for safety we should set up that fund, after all. I couldn't believe it. I hadn't seen him this reasonable or rational in years."

"So what happened?"

"Nothing. That was just it. We were sitting there in the reception area talking and he suddenly just went insane. Jumped up from his chair and started ranting and raving about how the lawyer and I were in cahoots and how we were going to take all his money and how I was nothing but a whore and how ashamed our parents would be if they knew how I lived. It wasn't anything I hadn't heard before. But then he started tearing the office apart, smashing everything, ripping out drawers, and flinging their papers everywhere. Then he turned on me.

"I'd been trying to get my arms around him, to stop him. But he shrugged me off and swung at me. He got me right in the eye. Then he went back to smashing up the office. Luckily, this was when Mr. Fitzmorris himself came in. He didn't waste any time. He took out a gun he had in his bag and smashed it across the back of Tim's head. And that was that. Tim was unconscious for a long time. I had a couple of terrible moments there when I couldn't find his pulse. I thought, 'My God he's dead. The whole purpose of all this was to help him. And now we've killed him.' I got a little hysterical, I'm afraid. Mr. Fitzmorris got sort of upset with me. Two lunatics in the same family. Poor Mr. Fitzmorris."

"How'd you get him to the hospital?"

"Mr. Fitzmorris ran downstairs and got a cab. We took poor Tim straight to the hospital. Halfway there, he came to again. He'd apparently blacked out. He said he had no memory at all of what had happened. That the only thing he could remember was coming up the stairs to Mr. Fitzmorris's office. Then he started sobbing. I think even Mr. Fitzmorris felt sorry for him at this point."

"The hospital give you any trouble?"

"Oh, no, not with Mr. Fitzmorris along. He's pretty influential, I think. He explained the circumstances and the hospital took Tim right in."

"How did Tim react to all this?"

"That's the funny thing. He was so violent in Mr. Fitzmorris's office. But at the hospital, I got the sense that he was really exhausted, that he was just sick of it all. He didn't say anything — not even goodbye — he was just very docile. The last time I saw they were closing this door on him — it was like a jail door with bars and everything. Now, of course, I feel guilty."

"That's not a very rational reaction."

"He's my brother, Dev. I love him more

than any other person in the world. Now I feel that I've deserted him. Just washed my hands of him. That's not anything a good sister would do, is it?"

She'd taken her veil off. I was still trying to adjust to the sight of that sweet, pretty face — every schoolboy's first crush, I thought again — wearing a black eye. It didn't look good on her. It looked vulgar, in fact. But it was also emblematic of all she'd done for her brother over the years. She had nothing to feel guilty about. Tim couldn't have asked for a more trusted or loyal friend.

"I'm going to visit him this afternoon."

"He'll be glad to see you."

"I'm hoping we can have dinner tonight — you and I."

"I'm hoping that, too. But so much has happened to me in the last twenty-four hours — I just don't know where I'll be tonight or what I'm doing."

"Well, if you'd like, stop by my room and we'll have dinner."

"Fine. I hope it works out."

She touched my hand. "I'm starting to depend on you. Push me away if you need to."

I squeezed her hand. "I wouldn't push you very far."

The next few hours were taken up by looking for where Kelly had lived. Turned out to be a sleeping room near an iron forge.

The landlady told me that Chief Yancy had been through the room twice and told her that he hadn't found anything useful. Maybe. If he had, he probably wouldn't have told her, anyway.

The best thing you could say for the room was that it was sunny. A hook rug, a spavined bed, a badly chipped bureau, and a closet barely big enough for two squirrels to dance in were the other highlights.

At this point, I wasn't figuring that Kelly had had anything to do with the deaths. But that didn't mean he didn't know where the plates were.

I sat on the bed and smoked a cigarette. Maybe he'd hid something — some kind of clue — and I just wasn't seeing it. Or maybe I'd seen too many mellerdramas on stages. In the outlands, mellerdramas were often the only places you could go to see pretty ladies.

I didn't find any secret hiding place. I finished my cigarette and left the room.

The landlady, a willowy Irisher with a

sad-dog face, said, "Did you talk to the bar gal at The Sing 'N Shout?"

"I guess I don't know what that is."

"A saloon down by the roundhouse. A very rough place. Pretty gal runs the bar at night. She came back here with him a couple times. He didn't know I knew, but I knew all right. But they were so lovely, I hated to spoil their fun."

"What's her name?"

"Liz is all I know. Never heard her last name mentioned."

"He have any other visitors?"

"Just the copper."

"Which copper?"

"The chief himself."

I wasn't sure why, but something sounded strange about that. "The chief? When was this?"

"Oh, couple weeks ago. Late at night. That was what was strange about it. And the chief was in street clothes. Wouldn't come in, either. They'd stand by that tree out front, on the shadowy side, and talk. You could tell the chief didn't want nobody to recognize him."

"Did they know you'd seen them?"

"I don't think so. I got a way of looking out the front window with nobody knowin' I'm lookin'."

I went back through what she'd told me. The chief. Late at night. Street clothes. Not wanting to be seen. It didn't sound like an official visit.

"He came a couple of other times, too, the chief. He had to come up to the door and ask me if Kelly was home. He looked real uncomfortable. He had a fedora and he kept the brim low. So I couldn't see him very good. He sounded mad when I told him Kelly wasn't here — like he was supposed to be here to meet him but Kelly went somewheres else. I didn't tell him about the boathouse."

"What boathouse?"

"My husband and a couple of his friends keep this boathouse. That's what they call it, anyway. It's basically just a shack with a long dock runnin' out into the water. Gets a little warmer come July, they'll spend most of their free time out there. They say they love to fish, but what they really love is drinkin' beer and tellin' lies about how brave they was in the war." She grinned. She had a warm smile that a full set of teeth would have made even warmer. "Closest my husband got to the war was the Rock Island arsenal. We lived in Davenport, Iowa, at the time. But to hear him tell it, he won all the big battles by himself."

"I believe I've told a few whoppers about my time in the war, too."

"You men and your war stories."

"You have any idea why Kelly wanted to go to the boat dock?"

"Sure. He was hidin'."

"He say from who?"

"No. But when the chief's son got murdered — Kelly took it real hard."

"The chief's son ever come around here?"

"A couple times. Late at night, just like his father. But he didn't skulk around. He didn't care if I saw him or not. He visited Kelly right up in his room. Didn't stay long."

"They fight or anything?"

"If they had, I would've heard it. This house, you hear everything that goes on."

"I'd like to see the boathouse if I could."

For the first time, I sensed her withdraw from the conversation, stand back mentally, and think of everything we'd been talking about. "You could be the one who killed him."

"I could be. But I'm not."

"Who are you, then?"

"We were friends and enemies."

She smiled. "Now *that* I can believe. Kelly was one of those Micks who could charm your pants off one minute and then make you want to shoot him the next."

"That was Kelly, all right."

"I don't suppose you'll tell me what you're lookin' for?"

I gave her my best open smile. "You're right about that. I don't suppose I would."

"Well, the husband's got the key with him. He works shifts and he's on nights this week. We keep meanin' to have another key made but —"

"I won't need a key, missus."

She put her eyes on me again. Hard. "I'll bet you know all kinds of ways to get into places without keys."

"I really would appreciate you telling me where this dock is."

She told me. "The funny thing is, I knew he was a crook of some kind. I'd guess that's what you are, too. But I got a brother the law is always houndin', so I don't much give a damn about helpin' crooks. Most of them ain't any dirtier than the coppers." She thought of something that made her give out with an indelicate snort of laughter. "He sure was good company, that Kelly. Made me wish I was young again. When I was young and I'd get all dressed up, I didn't look so bad. Kelly always reminded me of those days. He was fun to be around. The husband didn't like him much — didn't trust him is what it came down to — but I didn't care. He was just fun to be around."

"Yeah," I said, thinking of how Cora ran off with him. "That's what I hear."

Two

Kimble was in a meeting when I got to the bank. I told his secretary I'd be back in a while.

I hopped a trolley and paid a visit to Serena Hopkins. She wasn't home, either. Once again, my burglary tools came to good purpose.

The kittens greeted me. They seemed happy to see me. But you know how cats are. They'll fake anything just to get attention or food.

I moved through the mass of them on my way through the house. No idea what I was looking for, of course. At this point, all I could hope for was that luck would be with me.

If you ever want a good deal on bad paintings of ballerinas, I'd suggest you get hold of Serena Hopkins. The damned things were everywhere. Stuffed in closets, lined up against walls, stacked on top of a piano. And the thing was, they got progressively worse in terms of artistic ability. She'd hung the best ones.

The cats followed me everywhere, tiny pink mouths open in meows and cries. The only thing I had to offer them was tobacco. They might be able to roll their own — cats were even smarter than they thought — but I doubted they could manipulate the lucifer and get the cigarette lighted. Even cats have limits.

In the frilly pink bedroom, in the dusty bottom drawer of the bureau, I found at least one thing of interest — an outsize envelope containing train ticket stubs, a few menus from expensive Washington, D.C., restaurants, and three photographs of Henry Cummings with his arm around Serena Hopkins. Henry looked drunk. Serena looked serene. She was gorgeous. Not hard to imagine a retiring man like Cummings, dutiful husband and father and provider, being flattered into foolishness — and fatal foolishness at that — by a siren like Serena Hopkins.

There were other photos, too, the most interesting one being of Serena and the Police Chief of Denver, our own Clement Yancy, hoisting their drinks to the camera. Both grinned stupidly. Drunk stupid. The backdrop was some sort of casino. They had been there on a particularly crowded night. The place was packed with people who appeared to be just as drunk as they were.

I put the Yancy photo in the envelope with the others. I was already getting a possible overview of the situation. A simple one. Serena is in on the whole plan from the git-go, even going to Washington to seduce Cummings. But back here, where she's having a secret affair with the chief, she tells him everything that's going on. He starts killing everybody off one by one. Even his son. That way they have the plates and they can leave town when the time seems right. Now they had only to kill Kimble and Cora and they'd be able to get the plates ready for traveling.

I was maybe three steps outside her bedroom when somebody hit me. My first sense was that somebody had hit me with a building. The blow was that singular, powerful, and severe. I had just a few seconds to berate myself for not trying to do something besides fall to the floor. I didn't have the strength to pull my gun, slide out one of the knives, or even stumble away from whoever had hit me.

I just stood there for an instant feeling a headache of cosmic proportions begin to cleave my head in half with a rusty saw. I felt my senses start to go. I couldn't hear, smell, or feel anything — other than the pain. The machine that was me was shutting down. And then there was a gravelike coldness, and it was wrapping itself around me like a blanket.

And then I was unconscious. Or mostly so. Somehow, I was distantly aware that the tiny rough tongue of a kitten scraped across my forehead several times. And then I felt my wrists being bound in such a way that I thought my arms would be broken.

When I came to, I had a kitten on my shoulder mewling into my ear, two kittens asleep on my lap, and one hell of a headache. I was lashed to a chair, sitting in the middle of Serena's living room. The smell of cat shit was pretty bad, but was nothing compared to looking at those terrible ballerina paintings.

A female voice said, "He was actually a pretty shitty painter."

Serena said this as she walked into the living room toting a glass. "I'm just so vain, I can't take them down."

"Why the hell'd you tie me up?"

"Why the hell did I tie you up? Why the hell do you *think* I tied you up? Because you broke into my house. I was terrified. I still don't know what you're doing in here."

"I was trying to steal your ballerina paintings."

She laughed. "You're a crazy bastard. And I don't trust you at all."

"Is that why you hit me so hard?"

"It was just a piece of board was all."

"Gosh, a piece of board could never give anybody a brain concussion, could it? A harmless little piece of board." Then: "So you and Chief Yancy are behind all the killings." Long shot, felt wrong even saying it, but at the moment it was the only thing I had.

"What're you talking about, me and Yancy?" She leaned against the wall across from me. She didn't even have to try to look seductive. She just was.

"I found some photographs in your bureau drawer."

"Those? Are you kidding? Vince said I should get drunk with Yancy a few times, see if he knew anything about the counter-feiting. I went to three or four parties at the mayor's house with him. He didn't know anything and I didn't let him get anywhere with me."

"Untie me."

"Why should I?"

"Because (a) I won't hurt you and (b) if you don't, I'll get out of these myself. And then I really might hurt you."

"I'm not afraid of you anymore. You're big and sort of rugged and that part I like. But it wasn't even that big a board. I like men who can really take it."

"Maybe I could get hit by a train. Then would you respect me?"

She smiled. "I could blackmail you. Big, tough Mallory all tied up with little kitties crawling all over him."

She untied me. She couldn't undo the knots, so she went and got a long, gleaming knife. Deft she wasn't. She cut both of us several times in the course of sawing through the rope.

"You want something to drink?" she said.

"Guess not."

"I've got some sun tea in the backyard. That's what I'm drinking. It's good."

"Actually, that doesn't sound bad."

"You break into my house and here I end up giving you tea. I must be some kind of good person."

"A saint."

"I know you're being sarcastic. But I get tired of everybody thinking I'm just some kind of selfish slut. I've got a good side, too, you know."

"Every side I can see from here sure looks good to me."

"See," she said, "that's exactly what I mean. I try to be serious and all you want to do is talk about my body."

"It must be tough to be beautiful and have men throwing themselves at you."

"Oh, you're hopeless, Mallory. I thought maybe you were a little different. You know, the way I knocked you out so fast when I hit you with this."

She reached behind a chair and grabbed something. A baseball bat magically appeared in her left hand. "Just a piece of board."

"That's a ball bat."

"Same difference."

"You could kill somebody with that."

"Well, I was careful not to kill you, wasn't I?"

"Some 'piece of board.' "

"You wait here. I'll get you that sun tea. That'll make you feel better."

I spent the next few minutes rubbing my wrists. I'd been tied up long enough for the ropes to have left deep grooves in my skin. Every time my headache pulsed, I started thinking some pretty ungallant thoughts. Like taking the ball bat and giving her a taste of it. I was getting cranky.

Because I wasn't in the best physical condition at the moment, the sound didn't convey its exact nature to my brain right away. I recognized the sound as being improper in a town setting like this, as being dangerous in a town setting like this, and as conveying trouble in a town setting like this.

The scream helped. The scream sent my brain all the information I needed to get up off the chair and race to the back porch and then into the backyard, which was defined by small woods on three sides.

A gunshot. Serena screaming.

Then Serena not screaming, just lying facedown next to a small garden of flippantly colored summer flowers.

I had a pretty good idea — dread — that she was dead.

A bit of color in the woods — a light blue. Rustling in the underbrush. Footsteps slapping on a path.

"It's a good thing I bent down all of a sudden to grab a handful of weeds," she said.

Serena rolled over and sat up, brushing garden dirt off her as she did so. She didn't act or look especially nervous. "It came damned close, though."

I reached down and took her hand.

"He get away?" she said, using me to pull herself to her feet.

"I think so. If you're all right, I'm going to go see what I can find."

"Be my guest, Mallory. Kill him if you find him. I don't care about the plates or the money anymore. I just want the killings to stop."

There was another one. The queer money scheme was now effectively dead. The only one who might still be interested in it was the killer himself — maybe.

The woods were shallow, the path narrow. The summer scents and the summer sun made the air among the trees minty and warm. I had my Colt out. I walked rather than ran. I kept scanning the undergrowth on either side of the trail. True, the footsteps I'd heard had been retreating in the opposite direction. But that didn't mean the killer had left the woods. This might be a trap to lure somebody to come after him.

I stopped twice because of noises I couldn't identify. Once, the noise was sharp enough to make me crouch next to a large oak. I'd started to sweat. My nerves were wound tight. The war came back to me. I'd been in a few battles. Not the military kind. The escape kind. Caught by the Rebs for an hour or a night, fleeing as soon as I could. But they always came after me. A few times with dogs. And a couple of times there were battles, long exchanges of fire. One time, I'd escaped the battle by jumping into a river so far below me I could have been killed just by hitting the water. Another time, I'd escaped when some Union soldiers heard the gunfire — this was in northernmost Missouri where blue and gray kept exchanging dominance — and saved my ass. But the circumstances didn't matter. Nor did time of day, type of terrain, or even the type of weather. Gun battles were always the same — ask any truthful ex-soldier — gut-churning, bowel-loosening, sweat-inducing sieges of body and soul.

I waited, but I didn't hear anything else after a sufficient time so I moved again. Off to the west side of the trail, I saw that light blue color again. I could see only an edge of it, like a sample fabric in a general store. There was some kind of slant in the ground, beneath a large hardwood that had been cracked in half by lightning some years ago. I wondered again about a trap. I keep creeping forward, eager to find out what the hell it is, and —

For the first time, I thought maybe there were two of them. One a decoy to entice me forward, another a shooter in hiding, ready to relieve me of my life.

The raccoon solved my dilemma. Raccoons have managed to survive because they're smart. They don't often get tricked into human traps. This raccoon, a portly fellow now that summer had again made the pickings good, waddled over to the small patch of blue I could see and stayed there. If the blue had been a living human, the raccoon would have been leery. Unlikely it would have waddled over to make friends.

But not only had it gone over to the blue material, it remained there. Because of the slope beneath the fallen tree, I couldn't see much more than the rear end of the raccoon and the tree.

I crouched down and moved to the east side of the trail. What had looked like light underbrush was much heavier going than I'd imagined. Growth of every kind stabbed, jabbed, crabbed, and crimped my movement forward. On the other hand, the growth wasn't sufficient to hide me, just to make my passage halting. A shooter wouldn't have a hard time picking me off.

I didn't recognize her at first. I saw the head-shape of a woman with luxuriant chestnut-colored hair. I saw the light blue that was the color of her blouse. I saw the glint of a six-shooter in a stray beam of direct sunlight. But the pieces hadn't yet fitted into a revealing puzzle. They stayed just that, pieces, until I decided that if the raccoon could sit there unthreatened, then the woman wasn't moving. Might not even be alive, in fact.

The raccoon made good speed getting away from there when it heard me coming across the trail. At its size, it was comic to see. It made for a pine and deftly clawed up it in record time. It sat on a bough and watched me with great interest.

There wasn't much to see as far as drama went. After piling her purse and her six-gun on her stomach, I got my arms underneath her and started back toward Serena's house. I'd checked for a pulse. It was pretty strong for somebody who was unconscious from a blow that was now a goose egg the size of a baseball on the back of her head.

Serena stood in the backyard, hands on hips.

"Who the hell is she?" she snapped.

"That's what I'd like to know. She told me that her name is Natalie Dennis, but I doubt that's her real one. Let's get her inside."

293

Serena proved to be a surprisingly good nurse. She propped Natalie up on a divan in such a way that Natalie could stretch out with the back of her head above the arm so that Serena could look at it and wash it off. By this time, Tess O'Neill of the Secret Service — that being the identification I'd found in her purse — was muttering her way back to life. She was a bit disoriented at first, speaking words that might not make sense even to her. Serena got some water in her, and then gave her a couple of kinds of patent medicine, and then sat next to her on an ottoman and held her hand, listening to Agent O'Neill eventually babble her way into coherence again.

I said, "Serena, I need you to do me a favor."

"Oh? What would that be?"

"Go into your den and close the door."

"And why would I do that?"

O'Neill, who had only opened her eyes for the first time a minute ago, looked up at Serena and said, "For once, he knows what he's talking about. I'd appreciate it if you'd cooperate."

"You weren't the one who tried to kill me, were you?"

I'd been wondering about that, Serena's nunlike charity visited upon a woman who might just have tried to pump a bullet into her. I'd earlier told her that O'Neill wasn't the shooter, but apparently Serena wanted to hear it from O'Neill herself.

O'Neill said, "It wasn't me, Serena. I wish I could tell you who it was. I didn't get a chance to find out. He hit me from behind."

Serena shrugged. "I guess I have to take your word for it." Then, to me: "Don't take too long, Dev. I've decided to start cleaning this place up today."

I resisted the sarcastic remark that came to me. "It won't be long."

When I heard the den door close far down the hall off the living room, I said in a quiet voice, "What the hell is the Secret Service doing here?"

"I could be dying and you're asking me questions like that."

I mimicked her. " 'My poor brother is drinking up all the family money and there won't be any left over for me to travel around the country and lie to people.' "

With a pained expression on her pretty face, she laughed. "God, I hope I don't sound like that."

"There are certain people in Washington

295

who aren't going to be very happy when I tell them you've been following me."

A radiant smile — radiant considering the back of her head. "And you didn't find out until just now. I was with you all the way from Washington. My boss will gloat when he tells your boss. And why are you complaining about the Secret Service? You're part of it."

"A special part of it. Not your part."

" 'A special part.' Sounds pretty fancy," she smirked.

"I don't suppose you've learned anything on your own," I said.

"Why, Agent Mallory, are you suggesting we swap information?"

"You follow me around and let me take all the chances, but you don't develop anything on your own. So much for the Secret Service."

"Well," she said, and she was damned coy for being in pain, "I know one thing you don't know."

"And I don't suppose I *get* to know it."

"You might. If you promise not to tell you found out who I was. I'm not going to tell my boss about our little meeting in the woods. If you don't tell your boss, then I'll tell you what I found out."

I was having man problems again, that

duality of our nature that allows us, while dealing with an imminent problem, to pause at a crisis point and appreciate a good-looking woman who happens to be passing by.

I was trying to concentrate on being righteously angry about being followed, but at the same time I was also trying to concentrate on the nice sweet body stretched out before me. And that almost aggravatingly pretty face of hers. Much as I lusted after goddesses like Serena — and, face it, Cora — it was the women like Tess who interested me these days. Somebody you could talk to afterward; maybe even make a few plans with. Even if she was a Secret Service agent.

"I guess I could do that," I said.

"I don't have any right to say this, Dev, since I've been lying to you all along. But I love this job. If they found out that you figured out who I was —"

I rolled a cigarette. "So what did you find out?"

"You haven't given me your word yet."

"I'm going to make it contingent on what you tell me."

She started to sit up in anger, but then the pain grabbed her and slammed her back against the arm of the divan. "That's crazy. Nobody'd go along with that."

"You will. Unless you want me to let your boss know that I found out you've been following me."

There were all sorts of problems here. I'd have to tell my own boss, no matter what Tess and I agreed to. Our secret agency was obviously secret no more. It would have to be reconfigured in some way, newly hidden under a new name and a new protocol. There would also have to be an investigation about how we'd been found out. Nothing stays secret for long in Washington. But this was not going to make the President happy. It would make the Boss even less so.

"Well, it's up to you, Tess. If I think the information's worthwhile, you've got yourself a deal."

"Of course it's worthwhile. I know where the plates are." Then: "Damn this head. I've never had a headache like this before."

I said, "You mean you know this for sure?"

"Well, I'm pretty sure."

"Pretty sure won't buy you even a cup of coffee. Let alone me keeping my mouth shut."

She lay unmoving, hands at her sides.

"Are you in a trance?" I said.

"No. I'm just damned mad is what I am. I tell you I'm pretty sure I know where the plates are and you don't seem excited at all."

" 'Pretty sure' doesn't mean a damned thing."

"Well, I saw him on the roof. And he had something about the size of the plates wrapped in newspapers. And he set them down inside the chimney somehow."

"Who are we talking about?"

"Who do you think we're talking about, Dev? You mean you haven't figured it out yet?"

"Apparently not. So forget the bullshit and just tell me what you know. Or think you know."

"Chief Yancy. I spent a little time following everybody on your list around."

"How'd you know about my list?"

"I broke into your room. Several times, in fact."

"So Yancy's on his roof. Maybe a bird or something was caught in the chimney. They can make a hell of a noise when they do that."

"It was nearly midnight. There was a full moon. I could see things pretty well. And there wasn't any bird."

"When was this?"

"The day after his son was killed."

"If you thought the plates were up there, why didn't you get them yourself?"

"Because I never got the chance." More pain; she moaned, touched the back of her hand to her forehead with great drama. "Oh, God, just shoot me."

I put the barrel of my Colt to her temple. "With pleasure."

"Very funny, Dev. I really am in misery."

"And well-deserved misery, too. Breaking into my room like that. I thought you Secret Service people had ethics. That's what your boss is always braying about to the newspapers, anyway. What a bunch of brave, saintly folks you people are." I smiled at her. "You ought to be ashamed of yourself."

"Oh, I am, Dev. I'm terribly ashamed of myself." She tried to grin, but ended up wincing. Then: "That's why I stood you up the other night. While you were waiting for me downstairs, I was in your room going through your things."

I winced, too. My own headache had come back.

"Hey!" Serena shouted from down the hall. "I'm not going to wait in here much longer. This is my house!"

I stood up.

"Where're you going?" Tess asked.

"Where else would I be going? To check out that chimney."

"Then I'm going with you."

"You wouldn't last half a block."

"Oh? You just watch me."

She put a few toes on the floor and then a few others. Then she swiveled around on that nice bottom of hers a little bit and began the task of standing up. If her head felt anything like mine — and I was pretty sure it did — this was going to take a while.

"You could always help me up, you know, Dev."

"I just want you to understand that you shouldn't be doing this in the first place."

"Big, brave Dev gets swatted on the head and it's just fine for him to wobble around. But let Tess try it and big, brave Dev goes all manly on her."

"I just don't want you to get hurt is all."

"You just don't want me to get credit is all, you mean."

"That's the deal you wanted. I don't tell anybody anything about you, remember? So if I go get the plates — on the unlikely chance that they're there at all — then I can hardly mention that you gave me the tip, can I?"

She stood up in a single awkward motion and fell forward into my arms. She felt very good in my arms. I didn't even try and push her away.

"I suppose you're smirking about now," she said.

"Why don't you look up and see?"

"If I look up, my head'll start pounding again."

"Ah."

"I'm going with you, Dev."

There wasn't much point in making her any more miserable. She was going even if her limbs started falling off. She had that kind of female pride, which I admired but would never admit to admiring. Women have too much of an advantage already. If they know we admire them, things will really start getting out of hand.

And then she went and did the damned dumbest thing of all. She made a startled little sound and jerked her head back. I saw it before she did. Blood trickling down out of one nostril. All of a sudden her irises didn't look all that good, either.

I guessed I liked her more than I'd realized because when I saw her there like that, my stomach started to knock and my heart rate increased. This didn't look good at all.

She'd been hit much harder than either of us had realized.

"Serena!" I shouted.

"What?"

"Will you come out here, please?"

"It's about damned time."

And just as she was saying that, I glanced down at Tess. Her eyelids fluttered and closed. The tension in her body lessened. And then her right arm flopped downward. She was unconscious.

Serena came in just in time to help me get her back to the divan.

"She doesn't look so good."

"No, she doesn't."

"There's a doc a couple of blocks down. I'll go get him."

"Thanks, Serena."

I sat by Tess. I didn't talk to her or try to wake her up in any way. I had no idea what her condition was, but I didn't want to make it any worse.

Serena was back, breathless, in a few minutes. She bent over slightly to study Tess's face.

"He wants to get his buggy hitched. He's got a house call soon as he leaves here." She peered down at Tess. "How's she doing?"

"Nothing's changed."

"That must've been a hell of a hard swat she got."

"Must've been."

Serena stood up straight again and said, "You must like her."

"Why's that?"

"Your voice. It's a lot gentler than I've ever heard."

"Maybe so."

"She's a pretty little thing. Delicate. I've always wanted to be like that. Delicate, I mean."

I smiled up at her from the ottoman. "And she's probably always wished she looked more like you. That goddess look of yours."

"When it goes, honey, it's going to go fast. That's the problem with looking like a goddess. Now this one —" She nodded at Tess. "She'll be looking pretty and proper when she's ninety. You want good looks, those're the kind to have. Believe me."

The doctor was a skinny boy-man with an Adam's apple like a closed fist. There was something gruesome about watching him swallow.

He spent twenty minutes with Tess while we waited in the kitchen. I spent most of the time reassuring Serena that nobody from Washington was likely to pursue charges against her. No money had been passed. And as for Henry Cummings coming out here, he hadn't been kidnapped, just persuaded. There wasn't much the government could do against foolishness. When I said that, she smiled sadly and said, "I wish there was. In fact, there should be a law against it. I'd be all for it." Then she spoke a little of moving on. Maybe California. She said she was still young enough. And she said her reputation was pretty much working against her here in Denver. People held a special resentment, she said, for those who'd been born wealthy and privileged and then fell so low as to deal with people like Vince Kelly, and she didn't, she said, care if she was speaking against the dead or not.

"Concussion," the stringbean doctor said when he came to the kitchen door. "From what I can gather, I don't see any special problems. But somebody should take very good care of her. How'd she get knocked out, anyway?"

"Long story," I said.

He wasn't happy with the answer. "I'm trying to help her."

"So am I. And it's a long story."

He shrugged. "You're not being a very

good friend to her, Mallory. But I guess that's your business."

"I already explained to you that somebody struck her on the back of the head. I also explained that I don't have any idea what kind of weapon they used. And I finished by explaining that she didn't start bleeding from her nose for maybe half an hour after she got knocked out. I don't see what else would be useful to you."

"The police like to know about these things," he said. "There could be charges."

"I couldn't help you if I wanted to," I said. "Serena and I weren't anywhere around her when she got hit."

He nodded at Serena. "You can drop off the payment at my office any time."

"Thanks, Doc," she said. Then, when he was gone: "Why'd you have to be so snippy with him?"

"Because he was so damned nosy, that's why. He didn't need to know anything more than I told him. But he's all full of himself with his medical degree and thinks he can push anybody around he wants to."

"Boy, are you full of piss and vinegar."

"You would be, too, if you'd been hit on the head the way I had."

"It was just a baseball bat."

"Why do you keep saying that? You could've killed me."

She reached over and touched my hand. "You're too cute to kill, Mallory, though I have to admit it's crossed my mind a few times."

THREE

You can never get a trolley when you need one. It felt that way, anyway. I stood on a corner and waited for a long, long time. The only pleasure I got from this wasted half hour was thinking about how much satisfaction it would be to confront Chief Yancy. He'd been so clever. Until now, anyway.

The trolley was crowded. I sat next to a man who seemed to know the score of every professional baseball game ever played. He was laying out the season for me. Which team would end up where when all was finished for the season. I like baseball. There are times when I can even say I love baseball. This was not, however, one of those times. The old man didn't seem to notice this. He just kept chattering away, talking about obscure players and teams I'd never heard of. He spoke with such passion that silver spittle bubbled in the corners of his tobacco-stained mouth. And then finally, it was time to change trolleys and head in a southwesterly direction.

Yancy's house was a modest brick home with a modest yard and a modest number of shade trees lending the entire scene with a serene summer dignity. A copper in his position wants everything in his life to be modest; otherwise the town folks — and the press, of course, unless it's in on the corruption along with the copper himself — start to get suspicious. When I was a Pink, there was a chief of police who had a "summer cottage" that even Rockefeller would have been envious of. I hope he had some photographs to show the boys in the prison he ended up in. Convicts have a sympathetic attitude for crooked coppers.

Given the time of day, nobody was home. The street was quiet. An ice wagon was at the curb a few houses down, the heavyset driver yanking a massive dripping chunk of ice from the back of the wagon with his tongs and lugging it past the fascinated eyes of a lazy beagle. The driver whistled a popular tune. A man who liked his job, apparently.

I went to the back door and knocked, just to be sure that nobody was home. Then I went to a shed at the end of Yancy's clothesline pole and found what I was looking for. A stepladder. All this had to be done quickly. Somebody would see me and wonder what the hell I was doing on the chief's roof. And then they would get curious enough to walk to a police call box and inform the chief — or his secretary — of someone's presence on the chief's roof. I gave myself ten minutes for the entire operation.

The beagle must have gotten bored with the ice man because just as I was laying the ladder against the back of the house, I sensed something behind me and there he was. He lay in the newly mown grass, his jaw resting on his paws, his eyes raised so that he wouldn't have to exert himself and raise his entire head, waiting for the show to start.

I was on the second rung when somebody said, "You must be with the coal company."

She was probably in her early seventies. She couldn't have been taller than four foot eight or weighed more than eighty-five pounds or looked any sweeter if she tried. She was the Universal Grandma in her faded housedress with pockets and floppy slippers and beatific smile. She held a small plate in front of her.

"I brought these for you, mister."

I climbed down from the ladder and walked over to her. She smelled sweetly of sachet. Her skin was wrinkled, but her brown eyes gleamed with youth. "I always try and bring workmen something when I see them in the neighborhood. I can get you some lemonade, too, if you'd like."

"No, these'll be fine, ma'am."

And they damned well were. Two oatmeal chocolate-chip cookies with extra chips dropped into the mix. I was hungry, too. I thanked her very much for them.

She watched me eat like a doting mother, and when I was done and handed the plate back, she pulled a derringer from one of the pockets in her housedress. "There's something else I always do. Something the chief himself asked me to. I need to see some sort of identification."

I couldn't help myself. I laughed. "You're the toughest little grandmother I've ever met."

"I know. And it's fun, too. Ex-convicts are always trying to sneak into the chief's house, night and day. I never have figured out what they're after exactly. I suppose they just want to smash things up. Pay him back for sending them to prison." She had a great granny smile. "They don't figure that some nosy old lady like me could actually be working for the chief. It's like a dime novel. And it's a lot of fun." She gestured with the derringer. "Now could I see some identification?"

At any given time, I carry a couple dozen business cards. Some of them are pretty specific; others are more general. I took out my wallet and nabbed the DONE RIGHT card.

DONE RIGHT
There's only one way to do it —
the Done Right Way
Bill Evans, Prop.

I handed her the small card with the black type on it.

"This doesn't say anything about coal or furnaces."

"That's because our little company does a lot of other things, too."

"Such as what?"

"Hauling. Moving. We'll even paint your house if you'd like."

"There isn't any address or anything."

"That's because we're expanding so fast. We've had to take new quarters twice in the last four months because we're expanding so fast."

"Who's this Bill Evans?" She was a first-rate police interrogator. Her and her eighty-five-pound body and that bullshit little old granny smile. Some little old granny she was.

I gave her a mock bow. "At your service."

She eyed me, obviously not convinced. "And you're out here to do what exactly?"

"Fix the chimney."

"The chief never mentioned anything to me about his chimney."

"Well, ma'am, he certainly mentioned it to us. That's why we're here."

She handed me the card back. She was able to handle the derringer, the plate, and my card with no problem. She said, "Well, I guess it's all right."

"I'm just doing what the chief wants. What he hired me to do."

"Watch out for that ladder. It wobbles."

"I'll remember that. And thanks for the tip."

The warm granny smile was back for a return engagement. She was no longer a gun-toter, either, letting the derringer drop into her pocket. "I was serious about that lemonade."

"No, thanks, ma'am. The cookies took care of me real good. And I'm most appreciative."

"Well, like I say, you be careful on that ladder. Don't want to see you get hurt."

"You bet I will, ma'am. And thanks again."

The beagle had been watching and listening to all this. It had either drained him or bored him. He slept. An orange butterfly squatted on his head. He didn't even twitch.

The lemonade lady ambled back to her yard, and I took care to move slowly up the ladder, just the way she'd told me to. Sure wouldn't want to disappoint a nosy old bitch like her, would I?

The roof looked a lot steeper up here than it had from the ground. I'm not keen on heights. I once had to run across the top of a trestle bridge to escape some unfriendly folks, and I near froze when I made the mistake of looking down.

When I looked into the distance now and saw the gleaming city of Denver rising up like a robber baron's shining vision of godliness, I was just fine. I wanted to reach up and grab a handful of white cloud. I was a kid again and it felt damned good. Then I looked down. It wasn't much of a fall, but it was enough to make me dizzy, enough to take the kind of caution the old biddy had just suggested.

I inched my way up the steeply sloping roof. The sun baked everything, including my back. I slipped once and nearly went over backward. I threw myself to the roof and clung to the coarse wooden surface, my fingertips finding a few holes here and there to dig into. I stayed that way for a good five minutes, letting my heartbeat slow and my breath come back to me. I felt pretty stupid. And if anybody was watching, I had to look even stupider. The old biddy only had to take one look at me sprawled out this way to know that I had never repaired a chimney in my life. Hell, I'd never been on anything as high as this roof more than a dozen times in my life. The ground was fine with me.

The chimney was brick. Nothing re-markable about it. Santa Claus could never climb down it unless he went on one hell of a diet first. I grabbed on to it with both hands, hoping it would support me. I was a long way from being Santa Claus, but then the chimney didn't look all that sturdy. The smell and taste of burned coal played on my senses. And then the silty feel of air filled with coal particles brushed my skin like a kitten's tongue.

I reached down inside the square opening of the two-foot chimney. My arm went straight down, all the way up to my armpit. I felt nothing but empty air. But that wasn't surprising. What I needed to find was some flaw in the interior sides of the chimney, some compartment where the plates could be stored.

I was about to get damned dirty. I set to working. For the next half hour, I wiggled and waggled my fingers in every direction inside the chimney. The slightest jut of brick made me inspect it carefully. I pushed on the spot, I pulled on the spot. I found a few bricks that were loose enough to pull out an inch, but no more. I found a few bricks that pushed in a quarter to a half inch, but no more.

Every once in a while, I'd forget myself and mop sweat off my face with the back of my hand or forearm. I'd remember too late that I was streaking my face with coal dust. The sun got so hot after twenty minutes or so that I took off my shirt. None of this did much for my still-pounding headache.

What I wanted to do was crawl down the chimney. Inspect each brick on my downward passage. Find the plates and return them to Washington. The Boss would be happy. Until I told him about Tess. My impression is that the Boss's first marriage soured him on marriage. He had a lady friend from the Library of Congress that he took as an escort to various official functions, but I'd never had the sense that this was any scorching romance. Thus I had my doubts that said Boss would be too happy when I told him that I'd gotten my tip from a lady agent. Bad enough that she was with the Secret Service. But intolerable that she was of the female persuasion. What kind of a man took tips from a mere woman? A man, a real and true one at any rate, found his own clues. The rest of the speech you can write yourself, I'm sure. You've probably got friends who talk and think just like that. They're still back in their boyhood when BOYS ONLY clubhouses in backyards meant exactly that.

"Mr. Evans."

One of the many disadvantages to using a false name is that you don't always recognize when somebody calls it out.

Which is what happened when the old biddy from next door, unknown to me, came back and stood next to the loudly slumbering beagle.

"Mr. Evans."

At the time she called my name, my arm was stuffed as far down the chimney interior as it would go. I was having no luck. I cursed. Wiped more sweat off my blackened brow.

I didn't want to look as if I was terrified up here, but I did turn around slowly, my right arm clinging to the chimney.

She had her derringer out, pointed directly up at me. Now that part was laughable, the derringer. What the hell was she going to do with a derringer from this distance?

It was the other part that wasn't so laughable. On either side of her stood two old white-haired grumps in soiled undershirts, red suspenders, and tan work pants. By God if they weren't twins, right down to the bulblike tips of their noses and those burning blue eyes. Oh, and one other thing they had in common — they were both holding shotguns on me.

"This is Brice," she said, nodding to the one towering over her on her left. "And this one is Bruce. Needles is their last name. That's some name, isn't it, Needles?"

"Exactly why are you holding guns on me?" I asked, appropriately enough.

"Because if you don't come down with your hands up," said Brice or Bruce, "we're gonna blast ya."

"And you'd be blasting me for what reason?"

"Because you ain't no chimney man," said Brice or Bruce.

"Because we called the chief from a callbox after Mae here come over and told us about you. He said to hold you till he got here. He said you give us any trouble," Brice or Bruce said, "and we was to blast ya."

"I see. Well —"

And then I realized that I would have to walk down this steep-slanting roof. I was already afraid to let go of the chimney. I had a vision of my sliding down the roof and landing hard enough on the ground to break something. Maybe even seriously hurt myself. My head already hurt plenty. It didn't need another jolt.

Then Brice or Bruce stepped forward a few feet, and I saw that there was a way I could use a fall to my advantage. Brice or Bruce was close enough to land on. My own Colt was with my shirt on the roof behind me. They'd be watching me carefully. They'd be sure to see the Colt. And they'd no doubt start blasting away.

But a fall off the roof when Brice or Bruce weren't expecting it —

"Let me get my shirt," I said.

"Forget your shirt," said Mae. "You just come down here with your hands up."

I couldn't have played for my Colt even if I'd wanted to. I gave old grumpy Brice or

Bruce a long look. Brice or Bruce looked like they'd do a good job of breaking my fall.

I was halfway down the roof when the vertigo joined with my headache to make my passage even more of a problem. I didn't want to go careening off the roof and land face first in the grass. I needed to direct my jump so that I took Brice or Bruce down with me when I landed.

"Just jump down," Mae said. "And quit wastin' our time."

"He's scared is what he is." Brice or Bruce laughed.

"Heck, use the ladder if you want to, boy," the other one said.

I'd been hoping they'd forget the ladder. If I used it, I wouldn't be able to knock one of the twins to the ground. Plus, the way I'd have to turn around, find my footing on a step, and then descend — for some reason that made me more nervous than just jumping.

I had to move fast; otherwise Mae would start pushing the ladder idea, too.

The beagle barked. This should have made me curious, but at the moment my mind was fixed on jumping from the steep roof.

"C'mon," one of the lads said with a

laugh. "An' quit bein' scared."

I dove. I pretended I was jumping into a nice blue lake somewhere up in the mountains, just going for a sweet little swim, maybe with a sweet little gal right alongside me.

Brice or Bruce let out a piglike squeal when I collided with him. I hit him so hard I didn't have any trouble flattening him to the ground and grabbing his shotgun before any of them could quite make any sense of what was happening.

But then the twin still standing gathered himself, saw what I was up to, and started blasting away. He wasn't a bad shot, but then he wasn't a good one, either. His bullets ate up the grass as I rolled away so I could line up a shot and knock his shotgun from his hands. He got close enough to give me a couple tastes of flying dirt, but not close enough to hit me.

I managed to roll behind a lone, narrow birch and start to set up my first shot. But just as I did so, I figured out why friend beagle had roused himself enough to bark.

A familiar voice said, "It's all over, Mallory." And then a hard hard boot drove itself deep into my spine and the voice said, "You folks go on home now. I appreciate you being so helpful. Soon as I get this man locked up, I'll stop over and see you."

"We gonna get a citation like we did the last time we seen somebody botherin' your house?" This came from the elderly gent I'd moments ago knocked to the ground. You take most folks over eighty, Dev Mallory can whip them easy. Especially if they're thoughtful enough to be in wheelchairs while he's doing it.

"You bet," Chief Yancy said.

"I didn't get no citation, Chief," Mae said.

"Well, you're going to get one this time, and I'll see to that personally. Now you folks just go home and relax. Enjoy the sunset."

"It was a beauty last night," Brice or Bruce said.

"It sure enough was," Yancy said, adding a little folksiness to his voice.

They drifted off into the gathering dusk like children afraid they were about to miss something really special. They kept looking over their shoulders, longing glances back at the man on the ground with the chief's boot on his back. Maybe later the chief would douse him with kerosene and set him on fire. Now who'd want to miss something like that?

"Get up," he said after a long moment.

But just as soon as I started to push myself up from the grass, the butt of a rifle slammed against the back of my head. I felt blood seeping. I felt the tingle of flesh newly torn open. I felt the profound ragged blinding desire to take this sonofabitch and beat him until his bones were soup.

But there was so much pain, I wasn't able to figure out what he'd done. Pain occluded coherent thought. For a long moment, I couldn't even picture how such pain could possibly have been inflicted. Then a brief picture formed. Butt of rifle. Back of head. Collision. But making sense of it didn't help the hurt any. Bile came up in my throat, burning hot. I realized then that he was probably going to kill me. I was a *federale* and dispensing with me would put a certain burden on him to explain himself to the Boss. But he was a police chief, and a powerful one, and one who probably had a good number of influential politicians willing if not eager to help him out. It wouldn't be too difficult to concoct some story about how crazy Mallory decided to keep the plates for himself and then attacked the poor, naïve chief so Mal and plates could disappear into the distance. I doubted the Boss would believe it, but he'd have to go along. He ran a semisecret agency. If he pressed anything too hard — anything that might invite Congressional scrutiny, say — then he put our entire enterprise at risk.

Then the sonofabitch, the dirty rotten sonofabitch prick bastard asshole, hit me in the back of the head again, same spot, this time so hard that I was unconscious in an instant.

"I take it you were looking for these."

He sounded happy when he said this. When I managed to get my eyes open and saw what he was holding up, I should have been enraged. But I wasn't. I was hurt too badly to even be the slightest bit interested.

You've seen injured animals curl up into the birth position when they're wounded or sick or dying. I suppose they comfort themselves in this way. The cycle of birth and death, the fate of all living beings, the circle that none escape. I was sort of curled up into myself, at least mentally. I didn't even give a damn about ripping his eyes out with a pair of scissors. I was worried about paralysis and dying. My left arm wasn't moving any too good, and I had this strange buzzing in my right ear. I was bleeding from one nostril. And when I creakily reached behind my head with my good arm, the swell there was even bigger.

"There's some bourbon right next to where you're sitting. You could use it."

I had to force myself to understand the concept of bourbon. Oh, yes, alcohol. Relief of a kind. Hopefully, anyway.

I took a deep breath — as deep as I could at the moment, anyway — and opened my eyes wide.

Nicely appointed living room. The furnishings were all leather-covered. The framed paintings were of various Union colonels and generals he'd probably served under. There was a stone fireplace. A wall of books that actually looked read. A large hook rug on the nicely polished hardwood floor. And my friend the beagle.

I took the drink, all of it in a gulp. Then I made the mistake of setting my head against the back of the chair. I jerked forward as if I'd been stabbed. The merest touch of wound and chair had been too much.

The pain didn't go away, but the bourbon woke me up. I leaned forward on my elbows and checked out the small but very pleasant front room again. Something was missing. It took me a couple of silent minutes to figure it out.

"No photographs of your dead wife or your dead son. You're a sentimental man, Yancy."

He waved a dismissive hand. He sat facing me in the mate of my own deep leather armchair.

"My wife was a whore and my son wasn't my son. I was never exciting enough for her. She wanted to marry because her father, who was a stupid father, wanted her to do something with her very good looks except while them away in a frontier cabin kitchen. He did work for my father sometimes. My father owned the biggest timber operation in three streets. He did well for himself. Her old man always brought her along pretending she was there to help. She wasn't. She was there to trick me into marrying her. I fell for the trick. She was one of the most beautiful women I'd ever seen. I was very happy. She wasn't, though she never said so to me. Then one day, when her sister was staying with us, I found a letter she'd forgotten to seal and mail. The sister was explaining to another sister how miserable my wife was and how afraid she was that I'd find out someday that my son had actually been fathered by a young man who lived near her father in the valley. I never told her that I knew. I didn't want the scandal of a divorce or the laughingstock I'd become if people found out that Earle wasn't really my son. I'm willing to look anything but foolish. I'm not the brightest man, the toughest man, the most appealing man, as you've no doubt noticed. All I have is my petty little pride. So I stayed married to her as punishment. I knew how terrible living with me was for her and Earle. Somewhere along the line, she'd told him the truth, too. I think — behind my back, of course — he started seeing his real father. I gather they had a pretty good relationship by the end."

When he held them up this time, I took close notice of them. The plates Henry Cummings had made. "I actually found Cummings before you did. About six or seven hours before. And I found these."

"I'm happy for you," I said. "I hope all the killing was worth it."

He snapped, "What the hell's that supposed to mean?"

"The people you killed to get your hands on those plates. Arthur Davis, Earle, Vince Kelly. You've been a busy boy."

"I didn't kill anybody."

I believed him. He said it just the right way, I guess maybe that was it. Not exactly angry, but hard and sure in the way you'd say the earth really is round.

"I'll be damned," I said.

He got up and walked over to me. He brought along his fifth of bourbon. He also brought along the plates. As he was filling my glass again, he said, "I followed Earle one night. That's how I found out what was going on. He was talking to one of those kids from the center. The kid knew where Cummings was. I'm ready to retire. I figured plates would make for a nice retirement."

He'd set them on the arm of my chair. He walked back to his chair without taking them along. After he was seated, he said, "You take those plates and throw them in the river if you want. Too much blood on them for me. I've already handed in my resignation. Told the city council that I had some health problems. That's always a good one. Nobody wants to question you too closely. You know how people are. All those years as a lawman, I never took a dime. You can believe that or not. Then I get giddy over some currency plates. I don't do my job finding the killer because

I'm too busy finding the plates. Like I said, Mallory, all I've got is my pride. But as a lawman, I don't even have that anymore. I've got a sister in Minnesota. Lives on a lake. Freeze your balls off in the winter, but the summer's so nice it almost makes up for it. Nobody'll know me up there. It'll be a good place to live out my years."

"That's a nice little speech, Yancy. I even believe it. But I'd be a lot more sympathetic if you hadn't torn my head apart."

"I didn't know what you were going to do. I always could have shot you. Would you have liked that better?" He drained his whiskey. "I could use a cup of coffee. I've got some I can heat up. How about you?"

"I'll just sit here and be grateful you didn't shoot me."

"You're a hard one to like sometimes, Mallory."

He said that at just the wrong time. My head throbbed. "Look who's talking, asshole," I replied.

He laughed. "You sure on that coffee?"

I shrugged. "Yeah, well, what the hell. May as well have a cup."

I wished I could set my head back against the chair. But there was no use trying that again. I just let my head droop a little, the way it droops when you fall asleep reading, and in moments I was removed from the living room and the pain. I have no idea how long I was out. Probably not long. In a position this uncomfortable, it's hard to sustain sleep.

A sound woke me. I didn't confuse it with any dream. But I had no idea what the sound signified. I wasn't sure I'd ever heard anything like it. The next sound was easier to interpret. Something heavy hit a floor.

I had to orient myself. Track the sound and attribute it to an area of the house. It hadn't come from my left, which was where the bedroom was. It hadn't come from my right, where there was a small screened sun porch. It had come from behind me, where a short hall held a closet and the path to the kitchen. And the back porch.

I was now obliged to stand up. Under ordinary circumstances, this wouldn't have been much of a concern. But as I gripped each arm of the chair and pushed myself to my feet, I realized how shaky my legs were. I was experiencing real tremors.

No sound from anywhere in the house now. Distant voices from down the street. Humans, dogs. A cart clattering maybe half a block away.

A long suspension of normal activities inside the house. I couldn't even hear a clock tocking anywhere. Or the walls making their mysterious settling noises. I listened for some further signal from the kitchen. None came. A scent of pumpkin. Probably a pie stuck in a cupboard somewhere. Are you allowed to think about having a slice of pie and a cup of coffee when somebody is about to kill you? I had the feeling that the Boss would say no, that thinking about anything other than the threat at hand disgraced the whole mission. But then you know how the Boss gets sometimes.

I took my first baby steps. If I lived long enough, this is how I'd walk when I was a very old man spending my last days in some old folks' home filled with wheelchairs of dead people who suffered from the delusion that they were still alive because they had to pee every once in a while.

I felt for my gun. The kindly chief had taken it from me. I hadn't seen it anywhere in the living room. I wasn't sure I even needed a gun. An unreality settled over me. The only real-seeming thing was the pain. Maybe I'd imagined the sounds from the kitchen. I called out Yancy's name a couple of times. No response.

It seemed to take half a day to reach the kitchen. It was a small, boxy, sunny little room that smelled of spices and cooked meat. Cupboards, icebox, sink, table. There were framed paintings of the kind you see on orange crates. Really beautiful art that even the art-gallery types in New York had taken a recent interest in — lovely señoritas, fast-moving trains, field hands holding up fat oranges that gleamed like gold.

But my moment of artistic appreciation ended when I saw Yancy's boots sticking out from under the kitchen table. An oil-cloth twice too big for the table surface it had to cover almost reached the floor. Any other time I would have bent over to sniff the oil on the cloth. Always reminded me of growing up. Now wasn't the time for melancholy.

All I could see were the soles of his boots. Everything else lay covered by the cloth. I glanced around the kitchen. If somebody was in the house, they sure weren't hiding in the kitchen.

I needed to check on Yancy. Getting down on my knees was going to be slow and painful work. The throbbing in my head was going to increase three or four times over.

I began my deep descent. I took it easy, too. When I got about halfway down, I could smell blood and bowels. I was in no condition or mood to deal with either. There wasn't much question now about what I'd find under that oilcloth.

Questions came pouring in. How had he died? Had I slept through all the noise of murder? And not only who, but where was the killer? Probably already fled. But who could be sure in a circumstance like this?

My head began to crack open in two neat slices. I had the sense that my brains would soon join his blood and bowels on the floor.

There was a bottle of catsup near the edge of the table. I pushed it back so it wouldn't fall off. I lifted the oilcloth and peeked behind it.

He lay on his side, facing me. My eyes went to the wound first thing, of course. The wound that stretched from one side of his throat to the other. The way the others had died. Deep and deadly, the wound. Nothing tentative about it. Should I kill him? Should I not kill him? None of that. I didn't know if there was such a thing as a professional throat-cutter — who insisted on killing people only when he got to prac-tice his art — but if there was, this killer was it. Deep, deadly, no hesitation.

He'd always been such a dapper gent. No longer. Blood and feces had turned him into a mess. Drool ran from the side of his mouth. His brown eyes stared out at eternity with the look of a madman.

She moved like a shadow. Without sound. When I was able to push myself to my feet again, she stood in the kitchen doorway, a soiled red butcher knife in one hand and a six-gun in the other. The sweet Irish face looked as if cutting a man's throat hadn't affected her much at all. Her voice was just as unfazed as she stood there in the stream of sunlight, a working-class angel of freckles and prim mouth and impish grace in chambray workshirt and jeans.

Meet the killer. Nan Julian.

"I'm sorry for this, Mallory. You weren't in my plans at all. You didn't have anything to do with killing him."

"I guess we're talking about a man named Mitch Michaels here, aren't we?"

"How did you know?"

"I've been thinking about that possibility ever since I found out that Kelly killed him."

"He was my father."

"I'm sorry. But Kelly killed him. The

others didn't have anything to do with it."

"You're wrong, Mallory." She coughed. "Dusty in that closet." She adjusted the six-shooter so that the angle squared better with my chest. "He set the whole thing up with Kelly. He wanted as much as Kelly got. Thirty percent of it. He deserved it, too. But they decided to push him out."

"I don't think they thought Kelly would kill him."

"Oh, they knew, all right. They knew. They just didn't want to admit it." In those words her rage could be heard for the first time. "My mom ran off when he went to prison that time. My aunt raised me for the five years he was gone. Then he got out and raised me himself. People think because you're a crook, you can't be any good. But he was good, Mallory. With me he was, anyway. Nobody was ever kinder or gentler with me than he was." She lost her voice in her tears.

"Yancy didn't have anything to do with killing him."

"He took the plates. He was going to keep them. I wanted to kill everybody who had anything to do with those plates. If it wasn't for them, my dad would still be alive."

"He changed his mind. You were in the

335

closet. You must've heard him."

"It was too late. For him and for all of them."

"So you'll have the plates now. You'll be rich."

"I'll have them now but I don't want to be rich. I want to sell them to somebody and then go back to Ireland. They'll hide me there, the people from the old country. We've never had anything but grief since we came here anyway, the lot of us. I hate it here."

"That's some knife," I said.

"I honed it. Every day. I'd sit there and weep when I thought of my dad. And I'd sharpen this so that it couldn't possibly fail me. And it never did. It cut so deep and so fast they didn't even have a chance to scream. And the ones who were too big for me, like Earle, I used this gun. My dad's gun."

"And now you'll use it on me."

"Not because I want to. I'm really sorry about it, Mallory."

I knew what I wanted to do — the only thing I could do, really — the problem being that I had to move very quickly. And in my condition, very quickly was out of the question.

She raised the gun so that it found an

even better spot on my chest. I wasn't sure I could do it all well enough, but trying it was preferable to just standing there and letting her shoot me.

The first thing was to feint to my left and then lurch back to the right, grab the catsup bottle and hurl it at her.

"Hey!" I shouted. The sudden sharp sound surprised her. The gun got wobbly for just a few seconds. I lunged to the left. She fired. And while she was firing, I leaned back in the other direction and grabbed the catsup bottle. The swipe of it and the throw of it became one motion. The bottle collided with her nice clean forehead. Her own reaction was also one motion. She started to black out from the pain and fired off two rounds while she was struggling to stay conscious.

Now came the difficult part for me. Dropping to the floor, scrambling beneath the oilcloth, jerking Yancy's Colt from its holster, then shooting her a couple of times in the leg. That was the plan, anyway.

What I hadn't counted on was her gathering herself well enough and quickly enough to start pumping rounds into the table while I was under it. It was like a magician's act where swords are inserted into a narrow vertical box and you wonder how the sucker inside can escape death. Except this wasn't a trick and this particular sucker was writhing all over the place to avoid the crackling bullets.

I finally got my hand on the butt of the chief's Colt and yanked it from its holster. I'd forgotten that the oilcloth was so large that it touched the floor. Trying to find her legs wasn't easy. I just started firing at the area where I assumed her legs would be.

She returned fire a couple of times. But my fourth or fifth bullet did the job. She screamed and then started crying. There was a hint of insanity — all the rage she couldn't deal with — in her sobbing. And then there was just the dead metal sound of trigger clicked on nothing. She was out of ammunition.

She still had the knife. But I had two bullets left.

"If you try to run, I'll kill you," I said. "And I want to hear that knife of yours hit the floor."

"You would, too, wouldn't you, Mallory?" She was crying again. She'd reverted to being a little girl. Being an adult was a dangerous business. You had to face up to what you'd done. And she'd done some pretty terrible things, no matter that they'd cheated and killed her father.

I backed out from under the table on my hands and knees and then began the process of standing up again. When I was finally upright, I said, "Drop the knife."

"What if I won't?"

"Then I shoot you in the heart."

"You've already shot me in the calf. Isn't that enough? I'm a girl."

"You didn't show any of the people you killed any mercy. So I guess I don't have mercy on my mind, either. So you'd better drop that knife."

"What if I gave you the plates? Would you let me go? You'd be rich. You could live anywhere. And live the way you wanted." All the time she talked, she hunched over and tried to tend to her calf wound with her good hand.

The knife made a hollow metallic noise when it hit the floor.

And then she collapsed to the ground, sitting there Indian legged and letting herself wail. "You think they'll hang me, Mallory? You think they'll hang me?"

But she'd killed too many people to win me over. There was no reason they'd had to die. Kelly, maybe. But not the rest.

I'd always hated killers who went pathetic on you when they got caught.

Again, "You think they'll hang me, Mallory?"

"I think they'll give it real serious consideration," I said, then hunched down to take a closer look at the damage my bullet had done to her calf. "Now shut the hell up."

FOUR

A newborn crying. That was the first thing I heard after Larry Kimble opened the front door of his manor house for me.

Behind him, three servants scurried about the hall, toting various things to the room they'd elected to use for the baby.

"It's a miracle how quickly it all went," he told me. There is one kind of tear that makes a man all the more manly, and that's the one he sheds on the birth of his child. I saw my father and both my brothers do that and I've never forgotten how moved I was when I saw their eyes gleam with all the import of the moment. In the course of our day to day lives, we forget what it means to bring a life into the world. There's nothing more important, nothing more profound. My oldest brother was an absolutely selfish, mercenary bastard. We couldn't drink together because after a whiskey or two I always started busting up his face for him. That was before he became a papa. He then joined the human race. Maybe someday I'll join up, too.

Kimble led me down the hall to the threshold of the large, sunny room that smelled of steam from the scalding water, herbs, medicine, and sunlight. The midwife was rocking the infant in her arms. Cora, pale but lovely, slept.

He led me down the hall again, this time to the den. We seated ourselves and smoked the Cuban cigars he would no doubt be passing out to every living thing over the next few weeks.

"I don't need to tell you this is the happiest day of my life, do I?"

"Not by the look on your face you don't. Congratulations, Larry."

Sometimes expressions can change faster than an eye can blink. He'd gone from utterly happy to stone hard grim.

"You have to know what I'm afraid of, Dev. You could destroy us — and our child. I w-won't t-try to insult y-you b-by —" He paused. As he had that first day in his bank office, he very consciously got hold of himself. I'd never seen anybody else with a stuttering problem be able to do this. His willpower had to be amazing. "I won't insult you by offering you a bribe."

"Good. Because if you did I'd have to

arrest you." I smiled. "She's dead, Larry. That's what I'm going to put in my report. I'm going to make it sound as if Kelly killed her. Nobody'll be looking for her anymore. She did what she did when she was a different Cora. I'm a lawman, Larry. I'm not a judge or a priest. If you folks can make a peace with her past, I sure as hell can."

I stood up and offered my hand. "There's a train leaving in an hour. I need to get back to Washington."

We shook hands. He gave me another cigar. "For the train."

I slipped the cigar into the breast pocket of my suit coat and walked to the door. Then I turned and said, "What're you going to name the kid?"

"Sara Jane. After my mother."

"Nice name. Say hi to Cora for me."

"Thanks, Dev. For everything."

The conductor was calling the last of his " 'boards' " when she sat down, a bit breathless, next to me. She was too damned pretty for her sake and mine and she smelled too damned good to boot. Plus she had a perky little hat on that made her button-cute in addition to prim-pretty.

"What happens if I get sleepy and my

head accidentally falls on your shoulder?" she said.

"I'll have to shoot you."

"Well," she laughed, "now that we've got that settled, I can relax."

The train started to move.

"By the way," she said, "my head still hurts. How's yours?"

"A lot worse since you sat down."

"You can't fool me, Mallory. You're absolutely delighted I'm here."

Then she went and did the worst damned thing of all. Took my hand and said, "I have a feeling we're going to be seeing a lot more of each other. You know that?"

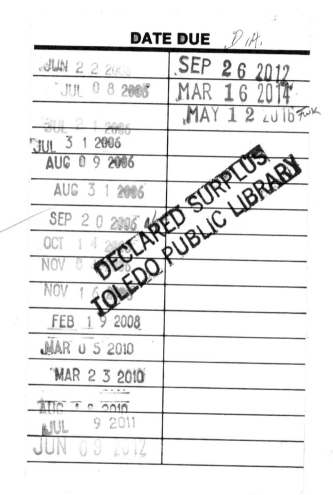